MW01492123

Kalina's Discovery

Return to Wonderland

CHEYENNE McCRAY
AND
MACKENZIE McKADE

ELLORA'S CAVE
ROMANTICA PUBLISHING

An Ellora's Cave Romantica Publication

www.ellorascave.com

Kalina's Discovery

ISBN 9781419958489
ALL RIGHTS RESERVED.
Kalina's Discovery Copyright © 2006 Cheyenne McCray &
Mackenzie McKade
Edited by Sue-Ellen Gower.
Cover art by Syneca.

This book printed in the U.S.A. by Jasmine–Jade Enterprises,
LLC.

Electronic book Publication August 2006
Trade paperback Publication December 2008

KALINA'S DISCOVERY

*D*edication

ೞ

To all the Wonderland and Return to Wonderland fans.
This one's for you!

Acknowledgment

A huge and hearty thank you to Annie Windsor, Patrice Michelle, and Patti Duplantis for your eagle eyes and making us work for it. Lots of love to you all.

Authors' Note

Return to Wonderland: *Kalina's Discovery* incorporates only elements of Domination/submission and BDSM. It is not intended to accurately portray a true BDSM or Dom/sub relationship. In the spirit of sexual fantasy, the Return to Wonderland series is also pure fantasy when it comes to sex. In real life, keep it real and practice safe sex. We'll keep those fantasies in Wonderland.

Chapter One

The sorceress Kalina backed away from the celebration of Lord Kir and Abby's joining ceremony. The room was filled with laughing couples and people in all states of dress and undress. Everything was colorful and beautiful, sparkling and glittering, just like the chamber in which the ceremony had been held.

It gave her great pleasure to see yet another couple having found one another—their soul mate—and to join as one. Yet as she watched the happy couples, there was a sense of emptiness within her that she could not explain. A sudden desire to be alone swept over Kalina, and she always followed her instincts.

When she turned to walk away, she stumbled into Jarronn, the King of Hearts and High King of Tarok. His comforting scent of an evening wind and sandalwood brought back a flood of memories as he caught her by the shoulders. She had helped him to find his mate, Alice, who had long since become the Queen of Hearts.

His smile for her was caring, but his eyes said he was deeply concerned about something. "Have you news of Mikaela?" he asked, his voice both brusque and worried at the same time.

Kalina sighed as she thought of the Queen of Malachad, sister to the four kings of Tarok. "Mikaela still runs from the shadows of her past. From what she has done and from the monster who was her husband." Kalina's stomach clenched. "No matter her wishes to the contrary, the Sorcerer Balin *is* still her husband."

Jarronn clenched his jaw as he released her shoulders. "Mikaela belongs in Tarok, not out where she could be harmed, where she is away from family. She needs protection until we can rid ourselves of the bastard Balin, and break her vows to him."

Kalina reached up and touched his cheek. "She has much healing to do. I am not sure she will be fully healed until Balin is conquered."

The King of Hearts gave a quick nod. "One way or another, the sorcerer *will* be destroyed."

Kalina stood on her tiptoes and gave the king a chaste kiss on his cheek. He had been her first true Master, and he would always hold a special place in her heart, as all the Kings of Tarok did.

"She will find her way home," she said as she drew away and grasped his hands. "Once Balin is gone, her demons will be conquered and she can begin to flourish as the good person she is."

King Jarronn gave a stiff nod and brushed his lips over her knuckles. Where once his touch would have sent her senses reeling, now she simply felt the pleasure of someone she cared deeply about.

He gave a low bow and released her fingers. "I must return to Alice."

"Of course, milord." Kalina smiled and watched the king push his way through the crowd in search of his mate.

Just as she turned to walk out of the enormous cavern where the celebration was being held, she saw Prince Eral watching her. Once again she felt trapped by his stunning blue eyes. For a moment she paused and she could not tear herself away from looking at the gorgeous man. Like Abby had once said, his flowing blond hair looked as though it had been spun with silver thread. She did not know what a Viking was—Abby had called him a cross between a Viking and an Elvin

Prince. But he was what he was. Werefin. Beautiful, sensual people of the sea.

His broad shoulders and smooth chest showed a swimmer's physique, his muscles well cut and defined. Like her he wore nothing, and she could not help but let her eyes peruse his trim hips, his powerful thighs and calves—and gods but he was well endowed. When she met his eyes again, his held a knowing smile.

Kalina took a deep breath, forced her gaze away from his and continued her path away from the celebration and into one of the long passageways. She enjoyed the feel of the smooth stone walkway beneath her bare feet, the cool cavern air against her bare skin. Her nipples ached with need. It had been too long since she had been with a man.

Her neck was bare of a collar, and her nipples were pierced but she wore no rings or other ornamentation on them this night. Nothing on her body showed the sign of ownership of any king. Of any man.

Not that she had minded being in the service of the Tarok kings. No, she had reveled in their mastery, had enjoyed being filled with one, two, three of them at a time. A slight smile touched her lips. She had loved being dominated and had been happy to serve as sorceress to the kings. She had been pleased to bring them their mates from another world.

But for herself…she was certain she would not find a true mate. She could not see her own future in cards, visions, dreams or stones, but she had always known that she was meant to pleasure and be pleasured, and to serve as a seer and a sorceress. But that was all.

Yet there was one man here—at this very place—Prince Eral, who made her body ache even more than any man had done before. But she had not acted upon the need he stirred within her. During the short time Kalina had been in Lord Kir's realm, she had seen Eral several times and had felt more than a passing attraction to him. She had no doubt he felt that same connection, and he had even asked her to join him during a feast, or on a walk around the caverns.

She was not sure why, but during those few days before Abby and Kir's joining, she had refused Eral's advances then avoided him. She had enjoyed plenty of casual relationships in the past, and sex was as natural to her as breathing. But something about Eral told her she could become much more attached to him than she could to just any man. Not like a true mate, of course. The fact was she did not want to develop a relationship with a werefin. Not from any prejudice, but because he was a water creature and she was of the land. The two could not mix — it was not possible. She was a weretiger — she was terrified of water. He would always be a creature of the sea.

Her long black hair hung to her buttocks and brushed the top of her hips as she walked along the silent but glittering passageway. Lord Kir's realm was one of beauty, with something new to explore every step of the way. She knew she was welcome to stroll from one cavern to the next. Kir held nothing back, and his people were free and pleasant. It was not uncommon to see males and females mate in their human or were-forms in any of the caverns. Here, the people rarely wore clothes. Kalina felt more than at home because she had never worn clothing.

However right this minute she wished to shift to her weretiger form and enjoy the feel of the breeze ruffling her fur.

After a century of living, she had schooled herself to ignore the pain of transformation. Her body shifted, elongated, as did her arms and legs. Her features morphed into the strong face of a tiger. She was white with black stripes and her hair warmed her skin.

She paced the hallways, her powerful muscles flexing with every step. She moved silently for a while, feeling somewhat melancholy — as if there was something she might miss once she left this place. Soon she would leave to meet with Queen Mikaela again, to help soothe the queen's aching heart and her horror at what she had done to her brothers, their mates and their kingdoms while under the influence of the evil sorcerer Balin, her husband.

At the thought of that bastard, Kalina gave a low growl that reverberated against the stone passage's walls. Thank the gods that Prince Eral had saved Abby and Lord Kir from Balin.

Kalina continued to pad from one cavern to the next until she felt almost lost. It was a beautiful maze that smelled of rich earth and exotic flowers. She really did not mind not knowing where she was. She was a weretiger — she would scent her way back.

A shiver ran up her spine and her hair rose at her back. Her seer and weretiger senses told her she was being followed. She looked over her shoulder but no one was there. Kalina's heart raced a bit, but she continued her walk. The cavern air pushed against her face, so she scented nothing. But she had no doubt she was not entirely alone.

Finally she entered a cavern that stole her breath and made her body tingle from head to toe. This time her growl was one of pleasure.

It was a place of sapphires as blue as Eral's eyes. The chamber glittered and glowed, bathing the room in soft blue light. It was not a large cavern, but it was cozy and beautiful. At one end a natural spring flowed into a pool surrounded by polished granite, and short, mossy, grasslike plants extended around it. She slowly walked to the spring and felt its warmth flow over her. The moist air coated her muzzle. When she reached the mosslike grass, it felt like a soft cushioned bed beneath her paws.

Intent on enjoying the pleasure of a warm bath, Kalina shifted into her human form. She could almost visualize herself as her body morphed back into a slender woman with long black hair, full breasts, a shaved mons and amber eyes. When once again she stood straight and tall, she took a deep, cleansing breath.

There was no breeze in the room, so when she inhaled she noticed the slight salty scent that did not match the smells of sulfur from the underground spring.

Her weretiger senses went on full alert. Her spine tingled and she prepared to shift again. Now she was positive she *was not* alone.

She whirled—and found herself face-to-face with Eral.

How had he snuck up on her, so close without her being aware of him? Especially when she had been in weretiger form. The people of the sea obviously had talents beyond what she had been aware of.

Eral gave her a sensual smile, and raised his hand to wrap a lock of her long black hair around his fingers. He gave a light tug. "You cannot run away from me anymore, little witch."

Kalina swallowed but forced a haughty expression. "What makes you think I will not?"

He moved nearer, at the same time drawing her to him by tugging at her hair. He was so close now that his cock nudged her belly and her nipples brushed his chest.

Desire swept through her, swift and strong. She was more than wet between her thighs and her nipples were as hard as the sapphires in the chamber.

"I want you." His blue eyes focused on her as if she was the only woman he had ever desired. "Why have you been avoiding me?"

She let her mouth curve into a smile as she placed her palms against his smooth chest and felt his heat. "We are of two different worlds, you and I." She pinched his small male nipples, and he sucked in a breath. "You love the sea. I am of the land."

His hands grasped her hips and pulled her closer. "The water and the land always meet. Nothing can separate that or change it."

"The ebb and flow, the pounding of water against rock and sand will soon lead to erosion." Kalina released his nipples and slid her fingers up his chest to his fine, silken, silvery-blond hair that flowed past his shoulders to the small of his back. She clenched both hands in his hair and drew his face closer to hers until she felt his warm breath on her lips. "Far be it for me to challenge such a truth," she said just before she drew his mouth to hers.

There was no hesitancy, no holding back for either one of them. Kalina slipped her tongue between his parted lips and he answered with a thrust of his own. He tasted of oak mead he no doubt drank at the celebration. But there was more to him. A heady masculine taste that made her head spin and her body heat as if the alcohol flowed through her own body.

And his smell — gods, it was incredible. He smelled wild and free, of the ocean and crisp air mixed with male musk.

Eral's kiss matched hers as her need grew more urgent. He lightly bit her lower lip and she sighed in satisfaction at the erotic feeling of it. Her hands slid further into his hair until she grasped it in both fists and drew him impossibly closer.

His palms grazed her skin as they slid up the curve of her waist to her generous breasts and he held their weight in his palms. Then he took only his thumbs and began teasing her nipples by circling them, making them even harder.

The kiss was so luxurious, the feel of his touch, his body, so incredible that it took all she had to break the kiss.

When she did, she looked up at him, studying the line of his jaw, the height of his cheekbones, and the smooth skin of his people. He was beautiful.

Eral smoothed hair from her face. "You have the most amazing amber eyes, my sweet little witch."

She paused for a moment. No matter the warning in her heart, she wanted this man for whatever short amount of time they might have together. "Why not play until one of us is called on to other demands?"

He studied her then gave a slow nod and a sensual smile.

"I am in need of a bath." She skimmed her fingernails down his chest to his groin. "Do you wish to join me?"

Eral gave a low groan and caught one of her hands with his and laced his fingers through hers. He led her from the carpet-like, mossy grass to the pool where they walked down granite steps and into its warm waters.

Bathing pools or showers were natural to Kalina's human side. It was only great bodies of water that made her shake from head to toe. Lakes and seas petrified most weretigers.

The water felt cool to Kalina's heated flesh. Her body heat had spiked with Eral's presence and her own arousal. Why she had waited so long, she did not really understand. She would not suffer heartbreak because she would never love a man in the sense of a true mate. She loved every man she joined physically with in her own way, but she always let go with a smile of serenity. For her it was all about being pleasured as much as she had pleasured the man.

But there was just *something* about Eral that set her instincts on cautious alert.

When they were up to their waists, he led Kalina to an underwater stone bench. She waved her hand in the air and used her powers to summon her mint- and sweet-tea-scented body and hair gels.

He raised one eyebrow as the stone jars appeared in her hands and she set them on the rocks behind the bench. She then summoned two large, fluffy towels that were now perched on a huge flat sapphire a few feet away from the pool, next to the jars.

Before she could call forth a body sponge, a yellow one appeared in Eral's hand, which he set next to the towels.

Kalina tilted her head back in the water, wetting it then raised up again. She started to reach for her hair gel, but Eral stopped her. "Allow me." He pulled the large cork from the wide-mouthed jar and scooped some of the gel out with his fingers. He closed his eyes and drew in the scent of the gel. "It smells of you," he said as he opened his eyes again.

She had a difficult time breathing as he moved behind her and began soaping her hair from the roots, all the way down to her hips. "I love your hair," Eral said as he massaged her scalp with the pads of his thumbs and fingers. "I have never bathed a woman before."

With a sigh, she said, "I find that hard to believe. Your touch is amazing."

He leaned close and whispered in her ear, "You will find I have many talents."

Kalina shivered in anticipation and her nipples ached so hard she considered squeezing and pulling them herself to relieve some of the intense pressure building inside her.

Before she could, Eral tilted her head back down to the water. "I will rinse you now." His voice came out as a command, which surprised her. She had not seen a dominant side to him since she had been here, although she *had* been avoiding him.

She had thought having her hair washed felt incredible, but having her body washed by Eral was simply amazing, erotic. She was sitting on the granite bench, her body submerged to the bottom of her breasts. He turned her sideways so that he could reach her back.

He took his time, using the scented body gel, starting with her back. He had her hold her hair up out of his way, and he rubbed the sponge over her in slow, sensuous, movements that caused the base of her spine to tingle. She felt as if the yellow sponge had some sort of healing powers within it that relaxed her, made her feel more vibrant and alive.

He worked down all the way to the top of her buttocks and her quim ached enough that she would have touched her clit if she was not holding her hair up out of his way. When he finished soaping her, he washed out the sponge then rinsed her back before having her release her wet hair again.

Eral's beautiful eyes caught hers once more as he turned her to face him. The blue light from the gleaming sapphires caused his silvery-blond hair to be streaked with blue highlights.

"You have the most amazing body, Kalina." He put more gel on the sponge before taking one of her arms and starting to soap it. "Imagine what I can, what I *will* do to you."

Kalina cleared her throat from the thought of him driving into her, fucking her hard. But as many men as she had been with, as many positions she had been put into, how could he be any different?

He rubbed his lips along her wet jaw and as if reading her mind he murmured, "Because *I* am different."

The sensual promise in his tone, and his words sent a shiver straight up her spine. "What do you plan to do to me?" she tried to ask casually as she shifted on the bench.

"I plan to do a lot of things *with* you." He began soaping her other arm, starting at her shoulder, working his way down her arm to each of her fingers. "And you are going to enjoy every minute, every second of it."

Kalina purred as he started on her neck and slowly worked his way down to her chest. He teased her by taking the sponge around and between her large breasts, but not actually touching them. Her purr turned into a whimper as he moved down her flat belly. "I think you missed something," she said as he reached her hips.

He looked up at her and gave her one of his to-die-for sexy grins. "Not missing a thing I did not mean to miss."

She groaned and then groaned again as the sponge barely brushed over her shaved mound to her other hip. He dipped his head below water and stayed there. Bubbles rose to the surface as he paid special attention to her thighs, knees, calves, ankles and to every one of her toes.

Her heart raced a little faster, panic welling up in her throat at the thought of him being underwater for so long, and she had to force herself to remember that he was a werefin.

Panic was replaced by a feeling of sheer pleasure as the yellow sponge floated to the surface and he pressed her thighs wide apart by placing his hands on the insides of her knees. The sponge was replaced by his tongue on her inner thigh and she almost shot straight out of her seat at the feel of it. The water beneath her breasts caused them to float and she could not help but bring her hands to her nipples and squeeze and roll them as his tongue reached her inner thigh.

Just when she thought he was going to put that tongue on her quim, he moved to the inside of her other thigh, licking, kissing, sucking his way toward her folds. Her thighs trembled. Her body was on fire. He was right, nothing exactly like this had ever been done to her.

Just when she thought she could not take his teasing anymore, he grasped her legs with his hands and spread her farther apart. Her body burned and she released her nipples to reach down and feel the wet silk of his hair at the same moment he buried his head between her thighs.

Kalina cried out at the exquisite sensation. And when he blew bubbles on her clit, she thought she was going to scream. She was so close, so close to climax. But it was as if something or someone was holding her back. As if Eral controlled her orgasm.

His tongue lapped her clit and his fingers slid inside her core. She held his face to her as he licked and sucked, and thrust his fingers in and out while he rammed his knuckles against her folds.

She could not help her cries and the tears rolling down her face. In all the manners of Domination and submission that she had lived, she had never felt like this before.

"Please, Eral," she begged, praying to the gods he could hear her underwater. "I need to come. Make me come."

He answered by blowing more bubbles against her clit and her folds, thrusting his fingers deep inside her and reaching that special spot that usually guaranteed she would fly off the edge in climax.

But she could not. She knew somehow he was controlling her and she wanted to beat on his back, to rake her nails across his shoulders.

Instead she brought her hands from his hair to her nipples and started pinching and pulling them again, adding to the sensations.

She was suddenly rising. Closer and closer to the peak. Nearly there—

Eral moved his head from between her thighs and rose up, tossing his wet hair from his face so that water droplets splattered all over Kalina.

She could not believe it. Could not believe he had stopped.

"You bastard." She had never ever called one of her Doms a bastard, but Eral was not her Dom and she was pissed. It had been too long since she had been with a man. She needed to climax *now*. "Why did you withhold my pleasure?"

He braced his hands on the stone to either side of her. "Because I want to fuck you. I want you to feel what I can do to you. And I want to feel you come when I am inside you."

"Then fuck me." She was panting, her eyes wide and her hands clenched into fists. "I cannot take any more."

He grinned and grabbed her by the waist, picked her up and stepped onto the carpet of moss. She wrapped her legs around his hips and felt the hard press of his cock against her folds. Oh, by all the gods he was so close to entering her. She reached down to grab his erection and place it at the entrance to her core, but he easily moved her arm away.

Instead Eral eased her onto the moss. When her back was flat against its softness, he latched on to one of her nipples with his mouth, so hard she cried out and her voice echoed around the sapphire chamber. He used one of his hands to grab his cock and rub her folds with it. A final hard suck on one nipple and then he started sucking her other nipple just as hard.

She was wild in his arms, raking her fingernails down his back and clutching at his hair. She had never acted so animalistic for a man in all her years of being a submissive.

Just when she was contemplating murder, he placed his cock at the opening to her core and with one thrust, entered her hard and deep.

She cried out loud and long. Oh, gods, he felt so good inside her. Like he was swelling, expanding her, reaching deeper into her.

Eral gave her a smile of complete and absolute desire and need as he held on to her hips and started raising her up and down so that he was driving in and out of her. She dug her fingernails into his shoulders as she rose with him to meet his thrusts. Harder and harder he fucked her, until she was sobbing with the need to climax.

"Now, my sweet little witch. Come!"

Kalina screamed as her orgasm slammed into her. She tossed her head back and felt the full and complete throb of Eral's cock inside her, pulsating, pumping his seed inside her.

Her orgasm not only continued, but it was under her skin, flowing through her in ways she never dreamed. She looked down to see her skin was actually changing colors! With every drawn-out throb, her body went from purple, then blue, green, yellow, orange, red — every color of the rainbow. As every color washed over her she felt it to her very bones.

Then shock rocked her.

Not only did she feel the most incredible orgasm of her life but her tightly leashed magic threatened to burst from her like flames, consuming them both. Fear clashed with ecstasy as the colors continued to ripple through her. She had tucked away her powers for so long, so very long. It was heady, yet frightening to feel them rising to the surface. She had kept that powerful magic hidden from everyone—including herself—content to serve as a seer. But now—*gods*. She had to force it away before it was set free.

Finally, her skin returned to its normal tone, her orgasm gave way, and the magic dulled to a simmer then vanished. She was still sobbing from the exquisite feel of the orgasm. Even Eral's cock continued to throb inside her, sending small jolts of pleasure radiating throughout her.

She was so limp that when he looked down into her eyes she could only look up at him in shock and wonder.

"You were right," she finally managed to get out. "That was unbelievable."

He settled beside her, on his side, his head propped up with one hand. He used his other to trace small circles on her belly.

They just stared at one another for a long time before either one of them could speak.

Finally, Eral said, "From the moment I first saw you, I knew you and I would come together."

"Therein lies the question." Her body was too boneless from the beyond mind-blowing orgasm. "Why? I am a weretiger. You are a werefin."

"Why does it matter?" He brushed his lips across her forehead and she shivered. "I am free to come and go as I please. You are free to do the same. We can share worlds."

Both fear and sadness was in her smile. "I will never go to any great body of water. I am a cat. I fear it."

"But there is so much I can show you." He raised his head, and his smile was confident, cocky even. "It is safe to travel to Atlantis. We have special transport. Lord Kir has joined us often, as have other members of his realm."

"They're wolves, not cats." Kalina sighed and shook her head. "Let us just enjoy what time we have." She gave him a little grin. "I plan to make up for all I've been missing."

Chapter Two

ॐ

The mossy ground was a soft cushion beneath Eral as he lounged on his side, one palm cradling his head as he watched Kalina. A flicker of desire brightened the sorceress's eyes as she lay on her back so close he could feel the warmth of her skin. In the near distance he listened to water lap the shoreline and granite steps of the pool they had just bathed in. She was so different from most women. Independent and confident, almost as if she embraced a dominant side.

Impossible. She was of the Tarok kingdoms—well trained to pleasure a man. When he had inquired about her, Lord Kir had said she relished her submissive role. A role Eral had every intention of exploring with her.

He plucked a patch of moss from the ground and flicked it at her. As it skidded across her stomach and then came to halt, she rolled her eyes toward the rock ceiling. She brushed the moss from her belly. "Are you always this mischievous?"

His mouth crept into a half-grin. "Is that what I am?" He threw a leg over her abdomen and thigh, pinning her to the ground. "If I am mischievous, then what are you, Sorceress Kalina?"

"A seer." She trailed her fingertips down his upper thigh, a light and sensual dance across his skin. His cock hardened in response.

"That is not what I want to know." He caught her hand and brought her wrist to his mouth and flicked his tongue along the inside of it. "You are an enigma. A mystery to all who know you. I want to explore that mystery."

She stared at him for a moment then withdrew her hand from his, scraping her fingernails back up the path she had taken. His erection grew firmer with her touch. Was she trying to distract him?

Her gaze lowered. "I am who I am. I have served as a seer for nigh on a hundred years. What else is there to know?"

"Were you born in the Tarok kingdom?" he asked.

Kalina stilled before shaking her head, her black hair sliding over the mossy ground. She frowned as if debating whether or not to tell him. "I come from another realm. One I have not seen since I was a cub."

Once again he took her hand in his and kissed the inside of her wrist, but his gaze focused on her amber eyes. "What realm?"

With a heavy sigh she gave a light shrug of one of her slender shoulders. "It is far and I am weary of this conversation."

Eral watched her for a moment longer and decided not to push the subject—for now. Where *had* she come from?

"You said earlier you planned to make up for what you have missed." He cupped her breast and began to gently knead the soft globe. "What is it you missed?"

She glanced down at his hand and smiled. "Intimacy." Then her smile faded. "Mikaela and I have been somewhat isolated."

Ah...yes. Kalina had been with the Tarok kings' sister of late. He circled the sorceress's rosy nipple with his finger, enjoying the shiver that went through her. Had Mikaela been a bad influence? Or perhaps Kalina had been unattached for too long—she needed a Master.

Eral rolled Kalina's nipple between his fingers. Her dark heavy lashes swept her high cheekbones. "You have missed a man's touch—his dominance." He shifted so that more of his body covered hers, immobilizing her.

Her brows pulled together as if she thought hard on his question. "Yes. But I do not wish to be mastered any longer. I enjoy my freedom."

Oh, she does, does she? He casually brushed her words aside with a light laugh. Kalina was more than a born submissive, and he intended to explore that territory with her. His desire was to fuck her, dominate her.

She frowned. "You find something humorous in my words?"

He shrugged the shoulder not pressed to the ground. "Men dominate women completely. That is the way of our world." Then he tweaked her nipple, causing her to gasp.

Tension played in her jaws as they snapped shut. In a single breath, she said, "Not Mikaela's, not the Tarok queens', and certainly not Abby's."

The sorceress was adorable when she was unsettled. Her eyes were like molten lava beneath glass. Her small chin rose sharply. Gods, he wanted to fuck her again.

With a sigh, he rolled over onto his back and stared up at the sapphires sparkling in the ceiling, watching light and shadows dance across them. "These women you speak of are not from our world. The males in their previous world are confused. They have lost control of their universe, including their women."

"Mikaela is not from the same world as Abby or the Tarok queens." Her voice rose sharply.

He rolled back to his side, placing his palm beneath his head once again. With a single sweep he scanned Kalina's pinched face. "Yes, and this woman attempted to kill her brothers, their wives and their children."

Kalina narrowed her gaze. "As you know, Mikaela was under Balin's mind-control. She did not choose to do all that she did."

Eral dismissed Kalina's comment. It was clear to him that Kalina was misdirected. She needed someone to guide her back into their world of Dominance and submission.

And there was no denying it, the woman's heat called to him in an unsettling manner. It was like an undertow drawing him to her. With the unity of Lord Kir and Abby, Eral's own need to mate had been triggered.

Strange. His life had been one of pleasure with whomever and wherever he chose. The thought made him smile as he rose to his feet and looked down upon Kalina. Life was meant to be enjoyed — savored.

"Kneel," he ordered.

As if it was second nature to Kalina, she moved quickly to obey his command. Then a wave of concern crept across her face. Instead of casting her eyes to the ground like a good sub, she met his gaze head-on. Her amber stare pulled at him, as if a blanket of magic covered him, willing him to drown in their golden depths. He could get lost in those molten pools.

Yet he would not.

Mentally he shook his head. It was his trial to endure. Eral loved women to distraction. His father had said it would be his downfall. Still, he could not resist their allure, their scents and warm bodies, satin skin and silky hair, and their soft cries of ecstasy as he brought them to climax.

It was what he lived for.

His sac filled with blood, stretching and extending his cock. The pleasant ache was welcomed. There was nothing like being sheathed in a tight ass, stroked by a wet mouth, cradled in a warm quim, or having the taste of a female upon his tongue.

Yes. Eral loved women, especially when they were bound for his pleasure, as the one before him would soon be.

He began a slow pace around Kalina as she remained kneeling. She had a sensuous, exotic mien about her. He made a full circle and faced her once again.

With the wild ideas that were apparently floating around in her head, he wondered whether she would bend to his will. Or would she fight him as Abby had Kir? The thought held an excitement he had not known existed. Would he enjoy conquering an obstinate woman?

He was a Prince. Subjects bowed to his demands. Women fell at his feet. Whatever he wanted—he got. "Do you want me to fuck you again, little witch?"

Kalina's nostrils flared. Her puckered nipples did not lie, his words had aroused her. "Yes, but I will not be collared or bound. We will share in equal pleasure."

Equal? He raised one brow. What a quaint idea. Still it was only female fancies. The little witch deceived herself if she did not admit pleasure in being dominated.

Lord Kir expressed how Kalina enjoyed being ruled by the Tarok kings, not to mention multiple partners. Tension gripped his shoulders and neck with the thought of her being with other men. Why? He had no idea. Still his fingers curled into fists. "Hmmm…" he muttered, dipping his head side to side and rolling his shoulders to shake off the strange tightness in his muscles.

In the past he had strived for no ties—no commitments. His life was one of freedom and amusement. Lawl, his eldest brother, held the throne of Atlantis and the responsibilities that went with it.

Exactly how Eral liked it. His pursuits were of a female persuasion.

He was, for all intents and purposes, *the king's spare*—a substitute—should anything happen to his brother. Yet Lawl was healthy and sound of mind. Lawl was to marry a beautiful woman from the Kingdom of Incasha located to the far east of Atlantis' boundaries. The King of Incasha had been a lifelong ally with Eral's father, before he passed on. The union of Lawl and Mirus had been sealed at birth.

Unconsciously, Eral slid his knuckles along the curve of Kalina's jawline. "So soft. So lovely." The need to touch the sorceress was so strong that his anger rose. *What the hell is wrong with me?*

Lately, he had been on edge, as if his world was shifting. Several months before his father's death, his sire had berated him on his roguish ways. Warned him that the time would come when he would need to mate and settle down. With Kalina's arrival the intensity of his disquiet had risen to an all-time high. Whenever he was around her, he could not resist feeling her skin beneath his hand. She was forever invading his thoughts, stirring his emotions and stealing what control he desperately held on to. The air filled with her scent and it lingered everywhere, haunting him. Never had he lusted for a woman to the point it bordered obsession.

And not any woman—this particular woman—a weretiger and seer.

Impossible.

Eral refused to accept his father's words. "No," he growled in both frustration at his father and in answer to Kalina's stipulation to their further joining.

What was it she was requesting? Equality?

Kalina shifted to rise from her kneeling position at his feet. "Then we should part now."

The idea sent Eral into a mental frenzy. His pulse kicked up a notch. His nature to dominate rose to the surface like an air bubble released below water, fast and furious. No way could he allow her to leave, especially since he could not name this madness that twisted his gut.

Godsdamn, was his father's prophecy already unfolding? Was Kalina fated to be his mate?

Immediately, he placed his palms on her shoulders, staying her. "No." He released trapped air from his lungs in a single exhale. He would have this woman again, and then he would let her go. Prove to his father that destiny would not control his fate.

Kalina paused. Her eyes narrowed as she glared at him from her kneeling position.

His gaze remained fixed on her as a warm sensation eased through her veins like a slow-moving steam. The foreign sensation sent a rush of blood to his groin and a vise to clutch his chest and squeeze.

Gradually, he knelt beside her and leaned so close to her ear that his lips touched her tender skin. His tone dropped in pitch. "You are mine, little witch. No matter what you say, you want me." Beneath his hands he felt her tremble. Whether from anger or arousal he did not know.

The witch was his. That was all that mattered. The determination he felt disturbed him. He nipped her earlobe in frustration.

She squealed with surprise, but she did not move.

Was Kalina his mate? The thought continued to churn in his head, sending a shiver down his spine as he reached for a lock of her hair and twirled it around his fingers. It was cool and wet against his skin.

His hand tightened further in her moist hair, forcing her head back so that their eyes met. He could imagine her bound and spread-eagled upon his oyster shell bed, awaiting his desires. Her ebony hair lying against the opalescent luster of the mother-of-pearl would be a sensational contrast. Her heavy breasts rising with anticipation for the moment that he touched her would be breathtaking.

Yes. This little witch was his. The words felt so right—she felt so right.

"You are mine," he growled, daring her to contradict him. The light glow of the sapphires behind her created a blue halo around her. A smile tugged at the corner of his mouth. She might reject the idea. But he knew the truth—he felt it deep within.

Godsdamn. His father had been right.

Eral watched her throat move as she swallowed. "I belong to no man."

She had been christened a seer, a brilliant one at that, yet she was oblivious to the truth. He laughed inwardly. How blind are those about their own destiny?

He released her hair and stood before moving behind her kneeling body. With a swipe of his hand, he brushed her hair over her shoulder so his gaze could trace the sensuous flow of her spine. Then he closed his eyes. >From deep within he called to the sea for assistance. From out of nowhere a length of seaweed appeared, quickly winding around Kalina's wrists, pulling them together tightly behind her.

She yelped. Then silence captured the moment, before she spoke. "Remove your bindings." He could not see her face, but her tone was filled with a cool reserve. She offered no struggle against the rich green kelp interwoven with a stem of red algae. The two colors were a pleasant contrast against her fair skin. Two identical starfish clung to the sea plants.

Instead of fighting him, Kalina tossed her head, swinging her hair back over her shoulder so that it swayed across the swells of her ass. "I am free. No man's property. I wear no one's chains." Her fingers wiggled, gaining his attention. "Or algae." Her voice had turned haughty.

Inhaling deeply, he caught the scent of home, salt and sea life. "Remember, we play, until one of us is called away." But the thought of ever releasing her made his body tighten with tension. Everything inside him said she was his.

So this is how Lord Kir felt when he met Abby. At the time, Eral could not fathom the lengths his friend went through to keep his mate. Now, he had the beginnings of understanding.

Kalina held her head high, her gaze forward as if indifferent. He stroked his fingertips up one of her arms with a featherlight touch. Her breath hitched. Her confidence seemed to waver.

Could she feel their connection? Did she know the truth of their fate? How long would it take her to discover they were destined to be mated?

As he moved to face her, his cock jerked. Desire shone in her eyes. She swallowed, working harder to avoid his gaze. He cupped himself. His fingers wrapped around his erection stimulated him further as he slid his palm from base to tip and back again.

The lines of her jaws tightened.

"Does it excite you to watch me touch my cock?" He ran his thumb back and forth over the slick pre-come that appeared from the small slit of his crown.

Her breasts rose with each weighted breath. "Yes." Her response was abrupt as if it angered her to admit it.

Again he moved so that he stood behind her. Seeing her delicate hands bound with his restraints made his fingers tighten around his engorged member. The pressure was a poor substitute for her warm body.

"You do not wish freedom, Kalina. You need a man—a Master. You need me."

Her back went rigid in her kneeling position. Her body trembled. "You forget yourself." It was all she said. For the first time, he thought he heard her normally calm and serene voice carrying a hint of anger. She made no attempt to rise from her kneeling position.

He gathered a handful of her hair and brought it to his nose. He had never met a woman of such mystery. Mint and sweet-tea from her earlier bath caressed his senses. But there was something more—honeysuckle, strange perfumes, oils, elixirs and a host of other scents, including something earthy that was uniquely her own.

Even her independence thrilled him—but only to a point.

Let her resist what lies between us. Her surrender will be that much sweeter upon my tongue. This he knew to be true, because he was a warrior—a member of the elite Atlantis Marina within his brother's kingdom.

With a toss of his hand, he let go of her hair and released an unexpected laugh at the irony. "Freedom is only an illusion, my little witch."

Servitude to Lord Kir was what Eral and his family had insisted upon to repay the debt Eral's family owed the Lord of the cave-dwelling mountain wolves for rescuing their mother from Balin. Eral's obligation ended when he saved Lord Kir and Abby from yet another of Balin's schemes to seize Lord Kir's Emerald City.

Everything seemed so much clearer now. Eral's life had never really been his own. Even now he served his brother. Any day he could be summoned to Atlantis, and without hesitation he would go. Service was bred into him.

Freedom was indeed an illusion.

But the woman before him was not.

He plucked the two starfish off the seaweed wrapped around Kalina's wrists, and then he moved in front of her. Her cheeks were flushed a delightful pink. "We all belong to someone or something. For me it is my people, my station in life." When word reached the city of Atlantis that he was free of his duty, he had no doubt that Lawl would beckon him home. Until then he would woo Kalina. Show her the beauty of his world and make her his own.

"I—"

Her word broke off as he placed one starfish on her nipple. She gasped as the small echinoderm latched on. The suction immediately turned her pupils dark with arousal. Eral had a keen sense of smell. His nostrils flared as she released the juices between her thighs. A pulse ticked in his balls.

"Yes. You will enjoy my world."

As their gazes met, they locked into a trance that forced him to his knees before her.

"No. I will not go near the sea," she insisted.

When he placed the second starfish to her other breast she unconsciously leaned forward into him. He smiled and released the starfish, and then sat on his haunches before her.

"The sea is beauty beyond compare, Kalina. It rolls in to greet you and then pulls you into its embrace. Beneath its surface lies a different way of life filled with vibrant colors and more sea life than you can imagine. It is a world separated from the rest."

She was breathtaking adorned in the unusual sea life of his world. He knew the small creatures would take each of her nipples deep into their mouths. In his mind's eye he could see her rosy nubs tighten with delight, stretching and elongating with the pull of each animal's force. The pressure and vacuum was already breaking down Kalina's resistance. Her tongue slid seductively between her lips. She whimpered as he caressed the starfish over her nipples.

"I need to taste you," he groaned.

Hands at her shoulders, he slid his palms along her delicate skin, the action drawing him closer to her until their bodies came together in their kneeling position facing each other. A host of goose bumps rose on her skin beneath his touch. His firm erection pressed against her belly. He could feel the starfish between them, scratchy against his chest.

Eral captured Kalina's mouth in a fiery kiss to taste and discover her hidden pleasures. She jerked against her bindings. He wanted to feel her hands stroking his body, yet at the same time he relished her being bound for his pleasure.

A restrained woman held the key to a man's desire. It was fuel to fire. An explosion of power raged through his mind and body with such strength he felt the entire world was his ocean. He ruled everything in sight, including the woman under his command.

His breathing was labored as he broke the kiss. Passion burned in her eyes like none he had ever seen before. With a gentle swipe, her tongue slid seductively across her lips, as if she devoured the last lingering taste of him. The simple action caused his balls to draw close to his body creating a pulse so intense it was painful.

"You were made for sexual enjoyment." He ran his fingers beneath her chin. "You are my perfect match."

He moved so that he was lying on his back. His thighs were spread so that Kalina could kneel between them. Unable to keep his eyes off her breasts, he watched the globes swell with each inhale. His starfish clinging to her nipples were a heady sight.

Then he reached for her. "Come to me." He opened his mouth and released the soft, bewitching voice of his people, a lyrical sound used to seduce and enthrall. The musical notes left his throat and floated in the air to wrap around Kalina.

Her pupils dilated. She glanced at his hard erection and then captured his gaze with hers.

She wanted him. That was the first step to dominating her.

It was true that Eral wanted Kalina's surrender, body and soul. Yet he also wanted to show her the beauty of his world, the mysticism of his people. He lifted his voice once more using the melody to pleasure and arouse, not to lull her under his spell. Not as it would an enemy. A werefin's voice could be used as a passive weapon to mesmerize their foes, enticing them to submit peacefully.

Through half-shuttered lids he looked at her. "Take me into your mouth," he commanded as his hands slid behind his head.

This was going to be good.

Her knees were wedged apart to gain purchase, as she bent at the waist toward his throbbing member. The muscles in his abdomen clenched as he felt a brush of her warm breath across his skin. He fought not to fist his hands in her hair and pull her the rest of the way. With heavy-lidded eyes she watched him as her mouth opened and she breathed upon him again.

"Gods, woman, you are killing me." But he loved it. The anticipation of skin meeting skin, or in this case when she took him between her full lips, was a slow burn in his belly. A moment like this should not be rushed, but savored like a fine wine or succulent piece of eel. As if she knew he hungered for her touch, she lingered above him.

He tried, by all the gods in the heavens, he tried, but he could not take it anymore. "I need your mouth on me now." His hands came from beneath his head and he clutched handfuls of her hair, pulling her toward him as his hips rose. He did not miss the smile that graced her lips. She would pay for her teasing, but not before he drove deep into her warmth.

The breath he sucked in was a strained hiss, cool air filling his mouth. She closed around him and began to stroke him with her mouth and tongue in long, slow movements. He almost forgot to release the breath from his lungs. When her teeth scraped against him, he struggled to maintain control. But it was difficult with her trailing her tongue across the sensitive head. She pushed on the small slit several times and Eral thought he had died and gone to the heavens above.

"Release me, witch." His words were mere gasps. This was the point of pleasure-pain when he enjoyed the trip to the edge only to hang on to the precipice by his fingernails. It was also a rush to watch how Kalina gazed hungrily upon his cock as if her climax had been stripped from her. "Stay in your position." She obeyed his command by continuing to kneel, resting on her haunches as she leaned forward so that her belly touched her thighs.

He eased from beneath her and from his back to crawl to his feet. Then he moved behind her. Gods, her ass was beautiful. The palm of his hand smoothed over her soft creamy skin. From the moment he saw her he had wanted to part her cheeks and drive between them.

But she was not quite ready for him.

From behind her, he reached around to grasp the two starfish attached to her breasts. The creatures had a ticklish spot just beneath their belly and when pushed they would halt their suction. He found the area and pressed. Kalina whimpered as the echinoderms let go of her nipples. Her nubs would be sensitive, so he set the starfish aside and reached for her nipples. She cried out as he grasped each one hard, maintaining the pressure until her breath caught.

When he released her, she cried, "More." It was a plea he could not ignore. Once again he grasped her nipples. Her head was turned to the side so that he saw tears slip from her eyes. "Yesss..."

Eral knew that when he released the precious peaks again, she would experience numbness. An ache that would bring on sweet, sweet pain—pain that she would experience for the remainder of the day. "Each time you touch your breasts or brush them against something you will think of me," he whispered against her ear.

"Eral, I need you." Her words put a smile on his face as he held out his palm and a curved shell materialized filled with a cool, blue gel.

"Soon, my little witch." After dipping his fingers into the gel, he began to coat his cock, sliding his palm up and down until it was well covered. The glide of his hand released three quick tremors that raced through him from head to toe. He sucked in a breath through clenched teeth. Nice and slow, he eased the air from his lungs.

When Kalina writhed before him, he bent and nipped her ass. A whimper squeezed from her lips as she leaned further toward the ground to where her chest almost touched, hands still bound behind her back, spreading her cheeks wider for him as she knelt.

She wanted him—she wanted this.

"Tight. So tight." Dipping a finger in the gel again, he placed it at her rosebud. She moved against his hand as he slowly inserted one finger, working the gel inside and around her entrance.

When he slipped a second digit inside her, she cried, "Eral, please."

"You will not speak without permission," he warned, pumping in and out of her taut hole. He loved the resistance, the way her body clamped down on his fingers.

"Fuck me now," she demanded, her voice dropping in pitch.

Immediately, he withdrew his fingers. "You have earned a punishment."

"What?" Her shoulders lifted as she began to rise. He held his palm to the back of her head to hold her in place and she gasped.

Again he sought assistance from the sea. In place of the shell that was in his hand, a small red-beard sponge and a thicker piece of kelp appeared.

As she opened her mouth to chastise him, he crammed the sponge in her mouth. Her words became a jumble of sounds.

She jerked her head and he allowed her to shift from beneath his hold. With a couple of heavy steps he faced her. Taking himself in his hand he began to stroke. Long caresses that made him grow even longer, harder.

Gods, but he needed to be inside her. "Do you want this, witch?" He felt his eyes narrow as his hand slipped up and down his member. This game could not go on for much longer. He had pushed his limits.

She studied him then slid her gaze down his body to rest on his cock. Her jaws clenched around the sponge. There was a moment he wondered whether she would refuse him. Then she nodded and leaned forward once again.

Satisfaction warmed his chest as he moved behind her. Her desire for him was greater than her need for independence.

With a snap of his wrist the seaweed he held lashed the cheek of her ass. He would have her delicate skin a bright pink before he gave her what both of them wanted. Him fucking her — his cock buried in her ass.

The flogger struck her flesh and she moaned behind the sponge. His palm smoothed across the area. Gods, she was soft. He could not stop touching, feeling the light marks he left each time he flogged her. Again and again, he applied the whip to her tender skin, repeating the process of soothing her until she writhed beneath his punishment, crying softly around the gag. Cries that broke what control he had left. He had to have her now.

With a toss, he threw the flogger aside and knelt behind her. Her ass was warm to the touch, just right for fucking. Cock in hand, he nudged against her entrance. She pushed back into him as he slipped his erection past the first tight ring of her anus. He moved slowly, inching deeper and deeper until he was seated within her body. Then he reached for the sponge in her mouth and removed it. He needed to hear her sounds of ecstasy as he took her.

When his hands found her nipples and squeezed, a shudder shook her entire body as he began fucking her. He pinched and pulled and twisted as he rode her hard. Then he slid one palm down her abdomen to her swollen clit. She groaned low as he began to circle it. Over and over he teased the engorged bud. The muscles in her anus clamped down hard on him, almost pushing him over the edge.

She was so close and he was holding on by a thread. "Do not climax until I give permission." His toes dug into the moss beneath him. This time he would not restrain her orgasm, but let her control it. Only then would he know that she was bending beneath his will.

"Please," she cried as her clit pulsed beneath his touch. He jammed one finger between her moist slit working it in and out, fast and hard. Her breath caught as he inserted another. She trembled with control. He was so proud of her. Then he pressed his thumb against her swollen bud causing her to release a series of soft whimpers that acted as a catalyst. He could not hold back as he thrust once, twice. Her body quivered beneath him. Every muscle and tendon clenched. His toes dug deeper into the moss and soil as he braced himself. His climax exploded.

"Come for me, witch," he groaned, slinging his long blond hair over his shoulder while he slammed his body into hers. Then he stilled.

Gods, it hurt so good as his seed rushed from his sac, ripping through his cock and filling her ass. Simultaneously, her head snapped up. She screamed loud and long. Through his fingertips he felt her climax shift beneath her skin, the enchantment of the sea rolling through her like waves lifting and crashing against the rocks. He began again to pump in and out of her tight hole, flesh slapping flesh, while she squeezed the last of his seed from his member.

A rainbow of colors flashed beneath her skin as his essence combined with hers—and it seemed as if there was something more—something she was fighting to control.

But then Eral's heart hammered against his chest as he witnessed a dark violet hue joining the other colors. Concern at the sight of the dark color washed over him when he slipped from Kalina's body.

With a flick of his hand, he released her bound wrists and sent the seaweed, starfish and sponge back to the sea. He eased himself and Kalina to the soft cushion of moss so that they were facing one another. He captured her mouth with his and she was pliable beneath his assault. When they parted she graced him with a sated smile.

"Amazing." She snuggled close to his chest. The scent of sex surrounded them. "Do the colors have meaning?"

Eral pressed his lips to her forehead. "There is magic in one's release, especially if your mate is a werefin." He slid his palm down her thigh. "We rule the mysteries of the waters. A male werefin's semen is a catalyst that opens the pathways to a female's soul." Her eyes were big with wonder. Yes. She would enjoy his world. "The magic assists us in choosing our mates, determining their moods and ensuring their pleasure."

"All this through a rainbow of colors?" Her expression held curiosity. "Each color has a meaning?"

While his one hand inched closer to the apex of her thighs, his other hand brushed back her hair so he could see her amber eyes. "Red is courage and fortitude. Our lives are not easy. We must choose our mates wisely. Your red aura is very strong." He felt a flutter of pride in his chest.

Her fingertips smoothed across his arm. "Yellow?"

"Yellow holds the beauty of the sun, the promise of a new day—faith." He did not want to tell her, but this color was weak within the scheme of the color pattern she displayed. "Blue is for purity, of water and everything innocent."

She hesitated, before asking, "And what did my blue shade say about me?"

Eral's fingertips slid across her moist folds. "Within you lies honesty, at least as you see it. Yet you struggle with your own destiny. Are afraid to face the truth in what lies ahead of you."

"Liar." Her thighs clamped tightly together imprisoning his hand. And for the first time a girlish giggle bubbled from between her lips. "You made that up."

Caught red-handed. Okay, so maybe he did ad-lib. "Do you want to know what green means?"

She shook her head. "I'm afraid to ask."

"Green is for growth and rebirth, fertility."

Kalina turned her head refusing to meet his searching eyes. "Purple. What does purple mean?" she asked.

Purple meant turmoil within the being's mind and soul. Her hue had been very dark. "Come here, I need to taste you," he said, turning her so he could press his mouth to hers. As he kissed her, he mentally ran through the other colors that he would rather not see.

Brown meant change—the loss of one thing and the coming of another. Gray was indecision, unrest. He had seen light shades of these colors within Kalina's aura. But thankfully, no black. Black was a sign of death. Either death of the female or death by her hand. It was a color he had never witnessed while mating, and never wanted to see.

A clearing of a throat broke the two of them apart. "Prince Eral."

Dread rose in Eral. He recognized the man's voice at once.

It was time.

Eral looked over his shoulder at Klon, a fellow werefin and member of the elite Atlantis Marina. "My Prince, the King has requested your immediate return." The dark-haired man's gaze fixed on Eral's.

"Immediate?" Eral asked, already knowing the answer. His brother never gave any directive that he did not mean or expect to be obeyed. Although Eral was not pleased at Lawl's request, he respected his brother and served him. But he needed more time with Kalina.

"We leave within the half-hour." Klon bowed again and then pivoted to leave.

Eral rose to his feet and assisted Kalina to hers. He held her at arm's length, his hands caressing her shoulders. "Come with me to Atlantis, my sweet little witch."

A shadow crept across her amber eyes—fear burned in their depths. "I cannot." If Eral did not know better he would have thought he heard regret in her voice.

The knot in his stomach tightened. "You can. You must."

Kalina slipped from his grasp. She raised her hand to cradle his cheek in her palm. "We are not meant to be. Goodbye, Prince Eral." She turned and walked from the chamber, his witch disappearing from his life.

A kaleidoscope of emotions bombarded Eral. He had never felt like this. Never felt emptiness when leaving a woman's bed.

* * * * *

Lawl paced the throne room, his footsteps heavy. "I know of this weretiger, this sorceress, who is your latest enchantment." He stopped and eyed Eral. "Wooing her can wait."

Eral frowned from where he sat and returned his brother's glare. By the set of Lawl's broad shoulders, drawn so far back it made his naked, six-three frame seem taller, Eral knew something was eating at his brother. Was Lawl's apprehension due to leaving Eral in charge of Atlantis?

A wall of defense rose around Eral, but tumbled down just as fast. He did not ask for this responsibility, but he would do what was expected of him—for his brother—for his people.

Uncertainty touched Lawl's blue eyes as he spoke. "It is my duty to meet with Mirus' father and secure the terms of our unity. It is your duty to rule in my absence and leave this woman alone while you rule." Lawl's waist-length golden hair floated around his shoulders as he turned his back to Eral. A sigh littered with exasperation filled the silence as Lawl inhaled and shook his head.

Eral ground his teeth as he stared at his brother's back. Lawl thought Kalina was just another conquest. No, she was so much more, but Eral was not ready to admit it to anyone other than himself. He studied his brother. It seemed unfair that Lawl had not been given the opportunity to seek his mate as was normal for werefins. "It is apparent that yours and Mirus' is not a match made of love."

Lawl spun on the ball of his foot to face Eral. "What does love have to do with anything?" There was a sharp bite in his troubled tone. "We are royalty. We have a responsibility to our people—our ancestors." Lawl paused. He inhaled deeply. "It is time that we speak of the throne's secrets should something happen to me. I have delayed this for too long as it is. It had been my hope that you would mature and see the wisdom of learning to rule should such a fate occur."

Eral closed the distance between himself and his brother. "There is no need to discuss any of this further," he said sharply as he came face-to-face with Lawl.

Worry creased his brother's forehead.

Did Lawl want this union? Did he ever want to relinquish the responsibility of being king? Gods knew Eral never wanted the burden. Or was there something deeper troubling his brother?

Eral placed his hand on his brother's shoulder. "There is no fear of you perishing anytime soon. Besides, think of the chaos I would create with the crown." He grinned. "Just the thought of me ruling should keep you hale and hearty." He released Lawl and headed for the large oak doors.

"Eral."

Eral ignored his brother's call, as well as the possibility *he* would ever inherit the crown...he couldn't think of a worse fate.

Chapter Three

Ocean waves rushed up to meet Kalina's feet. Sand
swirled between her toes before rolling away again. Warm sun
heated her naked flesh and its reflection glittered on the
surface of the water. It had been a week since Prince Eral had
returned to Atlantis and she had planned to leave Lord Kir's
realm as well. She had thought she had other duties to attend
to.

The gods certainly had different plans for her for the time
being.

A slight breeze raised her black hair from her shoulders
and its soft caress against her ass made her shiver. Her nipples
peaked into diamond-hard nubs as she clutched an apple-
sized sapphire to her chest.

Wet sand clung to her toes as she stared out at the gentle
swells and drank in the ocean air. Since she was a weretiger
she had never so much as set foot into the sea until now. Like
any cat, she was terrified of lakes and oceans, and the thought
of being trapped in any great body of water made her heart
race and panic climb up her throat.

But this she could do. She could stand and let the water
tease her feet and feel the soft sand beneath her soles.

If only it were that easy.

If only that was all she had to do.

Kalina took a deep breath, her heart pounded harder and
she clenched the sapphire tighter to her bare breasts.

She was a sorceress, a seer. This morning her seer's senses
drove her to the chamber she had shared that one night with
Eral, the chamber of sapphires. Whenever she was compelled

to handle an object, she knew that once she picked it up she was destined to do whatever it was that she saw when she touched the item. In this case it had been this sapphire that had glittered as if golden light flickered within it, and had drawn her to it. The moment she picked up the sapphire, she had seen her task.

But this was the first time she feared what she must do.

This was the first time she wanted to run away from her responsibility.

How could she go into the water? How could fate deem such a thing on her? She could not swim and the thought of being in water sent her body to quaking. But she had seen her duty in the stone which forced her to take this journey.

"You have to do this," she whispered.

A larger wave crashed against her ankles and she took an involuntary step backward.

Just the thought of being with Eral made her nipples harder and wetness gather between her thighs. She could so easily picture the time he had fucked her. Gods, how good he had felt inside her, how wonderful it truly had felt to have him dominate her. How much she wanted him still. And those orgasms—nothing would ever compare.

She had thought she would never see him again, but now she had no choice but to go to Atlantis before it was too late. If only she could send someone else—but it was always her fate to deliver the prophecy or vision in person to the one who was destined to receive it.

"Are you ready, milady?"

Kalina startled at the voice of Derel, one of the werefins who served Prince Eral and his family far beneath the water. She turned away from the ocean and faced the man who was as naked as she. He was extremely handsome with ocean-blue eyes, hair as shimmering blond as Eral's and a scoundrel's grin. In his arm he carried the skin of a werefin. It looked much like the sealskins Kalina had seen during her recent travels with Queen Mikaela. Only the skin he held had a slight iridescent shimmer of a rainbow. He would don it once they began their travel.

Behind Derel stood two more men, each with werefin skins over their arms.

Kalina tried a smile but failed miserably. "You are certain this will work?"

Derel smiled, and she wondered if there was a hint of amusement in his eyes. "Yes, milady. Lord Kir has used this method to travel to Atlantis many times, and as you know he is a werewolf."

Werewolves do not mind the water so much as weretigers do. She took a deep breath. She could do this. "Then let us depart."

Derel bowed. He and the other two men walked out into the ocean then dove in with the grace of their species. In the next moment three mermen-like creatures appeared, except that each had a fin along his back. They were half in, half out of the water and one barked like a seal before all three dived below the surface.

Kalina brought her hands down and clutched the sapphire to her churning belly. She waited, and waited. The tension in her shoulders rose until she did not think she could handle it any longer.

Finally, a very large, clear, round contraption appeared above the water, pushed by the three werefins. It glimmered in the sunlight and looked for all the world like a giant soap bubble. Her trembling increased as she stepped deeper into the water toward the waiting transportation.

Her cat instincts threatened to take over. She wanted to snarl, to shift into a weretiger, to bound back toward the forest beyond the beach and run until she was far, far away from this place.

But she raised her chin, took a deep breath and continued to take one shaky step after another toward the bubble.

By the time she reached the werefins and the transport, the water was to her waist and she was almost ready to pass out from the panic threatening to consume her.

She took another deep breath, tried to calm the pounding of her heart. "H-how do I get in?" she asked Derel.

He placed his hand against the bubble, and it slipped inside the transport. "Simple, milady," he said.

That almost did her in. She was going to climb into a contraption that something could just press against and slip inside it?

No doubt sensing her terror, Derel said, "We will hold it for you, milady. Just climb in."

"But what about the water? Other things—" She felt something brush against her ankles and almost screamed. "They can just push their way inside, too."

Derel shook his head, his long wet hair sliding over his shoulders. "Once you are within its confines, the transport will be spelled and nothing can get inside. And you will not be able to get out until we arrive at the city."

The feel of the water around her belly was almost more than she could bear. "Is there enough air?"

"Plenty." Derel smiled. "Now step inside, milady Kalina, and we will take you to Prince Eral and King Lawl."

Kalina took a leap of faith and pressed her hands and the sapphire against the bubble. They easily slid into the transport. It felt like pushing her arms through thick gel. She took a deep breath and held it, as if she was going to go underwater, and plunged her entire body into the bubble.

That gooey feeling slid across her bare skin and it was surprisingly sensual and arousing. The moment she was inside, air stirred and she no longer felt water around her body. Cautiously she let the air out of her lungs and then sucked in another breath but this time did not hold it. The transport had a clean, fresh smell about it, like a well-scrubbed room with fresh ocean air swirling through it.

By placing one palm against the side of the bubble, she tested what Derel had told her about not being able to get out. It felt as solid as glass now. Somewhat comforted, she knelt on the bottom of the bubble and looked out at the beach that seemed so far away.

In the next moment she was underwater. She could not help but scream as everything went dark. Her voice echoed around the bubble and she hoped it was contained, that the transport was soundproof because she did not want the werefins to hear her.

Kalina's body trembled. She wanted to shift, to claw her way out of the bubble and back to the surface and the waiting shore. But she forced herself to calm down. To take deep breaths. To focus on what was around her. Calm. Serene. That was what she had always been.

Her weretiger eyes easily adjusted to the dark and she saw the werefins pushing the transport with their hands. As they moved deeper, the dark rock formations changed into lacy, colorful rocks. Fish she'd eaten on many occasion swam past, some in groups, others alone. Had the lone ones lost their way? she wondered. Several thin long snakelike creatures approached, slithering around the bubble as if trying to discover its contents. Her heart raced. The razor teeth lining their jaws might be sharp enough to burst the bubble, but a giant see-through mushroom-like creature drew the snakes' attention. She let out a breath of relief when they moved away in pursuit. The sight of starfish, like those Eral had placed on her nipples, caused her cheeks to warm. Her quim grew wet at the memory.

Before she even realized it, her heart rate had slowed and her terror had turned to fascination. The round sapphire felt warm in her hands and she found the inside of the transport was a comfortable temperature. Not too hot, not too warm, but perfect.

Lower and lower the werefins drove the bubble. It was growing darker the deeper they went, yet some of the rocklike things glowed and helped her to see. In the lower parts of the ocean, different varieties of fish swam than those that had been higher up.

She found the more she concentrated on the sea life around her, the easier the trip was. She could almost pretend she was on land.

The werefins pushed the transport toward an underground mountain and Kalina caught her breath. What if the bubble snagged on one of the jagged stones jutting out from its side?

The males nudged the transport lower and lower until a huge cavern appeared before them, a soft blue glow coming from within. Kalina rose up on her knees, leaned forward and placed her hands against the wall of the bubble. It still felt firm, like glass.

Before she knew it, they were inside the underground cavern and her lips parted in surprise and amazement at the glowing blue lichen that was bright enough to light the way.

She was moved through a series of caverns, all underwater, until suddenly the bubble shot up so fast that Kalina fell back on her ass, dropping the sapphire and bracing herself with her hands. They were half in, half out of water, bobbing toward an amazing city in a massive cavern. Atlantis itself was perched up on rocky hills and was as colorful and as busy as the sea life that had surrounded the bubble on the trip down.

In the water at one end of the shore, larger werefins cavorted with younger ones, their skins shimmering in the blue light. On land she saw many people going about their business, and all were as naked as she was.

When they reached a dock of sorts, the transport was pushed into a huge shell that was about the size of the bubble she was in, except half as tall. She pushed herself to her knees as the transport and shell slowly raised until she was just a step above the platform. She heard a clamping then hissing sound.

The bubble vanished.

Kalina grabbed the sapphire from the shell and jumped to her feet, her eyes wide. She forced herself to take a breath and was amazed to find it was like breathing in air rolling off the ocean. A clean, fresh scent that pleased her.

She was standing on the smooth shell now, the one the transport had been settled on before the transport vanished.

Kalina glanced up to see Derel in his human form again, but without his wereskin. He strode across the platform, took her by the hand and helped her step out of the shell.

"A docking station," he said as if reading her mind. "The transports dock here then the transport material is drawn into the shell to be used when it is needed later."

"Oh." She gripped Derel's hand tight as he helped her down the steps. She was surprised to find she was no longer wet from when she had walked out into the water before entering the bubble—not even the ends of her long hair were damp. She had not even noticed that the transport had dried her hair and body.

The werefin gave her a sensual smile that reminded her remarkably of Eral. "That was not so bad, now was it?"

She shook her head and this time she could smile. "Not at all." She grimaced at her next thought, though. *Although now I will have to go back up once my business with King Lawl, Eral's brother, is finished.*

But how long would it take to serve him like she had served those in need of her seer's skills before?

Derel kept his hand at the small of her back as he escorted her through the underground city. As they walked into it, the city seemed even brighter, cleaner, more colorful and beautiful than she could have imagined. It was made of seashells, and other things from under the sea that she was unfamiliar with, along with rock that looked like polished granite.

The city was not so terribly unlike the cities she had lived in, but instead of clouds floating overhead, only rock and blue lichen glowed brightly enough to help light the city. It gave her a strange feeling being underground and under the ocean all at once. For a moment, her chest tightened as if a flock of birds were about to burst through. Her heart pounded, but she told herself she had air to breathe and the water would not fall down on her head, crushing her. Slowly her breathing eased to a normal pace. She was on land. Way, way, way, below the ocean, but this she could handle.

People nodded to Derel as if bowing to a lord or a king. Kalina cocked her head and looked up at the handsome werefin. The sapphire warmed in her hand and then the knowledge came to her instantly.

"You are Prince Eral's younger brother, third in line for the throne," she stated.

He gave her a wink. "That I am, milady."

"Why did you not tell me?" she asked.

His devilish grin made her want to grin, too. "You have gone and ruined all my fun. Here you thought I was naught but a lowly servant to the royal family."

Kalina rolled her eyes and Derel laughed.

The path they took through the city led directly to a sprawling combination of buildings that could be nothing more than the royal palace. It was beautiful, the crystal blue of the ocean, and it sparkled like the sun had on the surface of the water before Kalina had left on her journey to Atlantis. Fountains of stone werefins rising from enormous shells lined the walkway. The werefins' hands were cupped, and from their palms rose the water that tumbled back into the fountains with a musical sound.

For some strange reason, the closer she came to the palace, the more it felt like a swarm of butterflies fluttered within her. The thought of seeing Eral brought a flush to her cheeks and heaviness to her breathing. That same feeling had come over her every time she had thought about him while in Lord Kir's realm, and those feelings had scared her. Like they did now.

Finally she and Derel entered the inside chamber of the palace and Kalina looked around in awe.

He brought her up short, but when he moved his hand from her lower back he let it slide down the curve of her buttocks in a sensual movement, startling her, yet making her nipples bead and moisture to gather between her thighs. "I will summon Eral," he said and gave her that roguish grin again before leaving.

Kalina took a deep breath and studied the room she was in. Gorgeous murals spanned the walls depicting the beauty of the ocean she had seen on the way down. In some murals werefins played, while in others they were in human form. Most were naked. Only a few wore any type of clothing. Werefins lived much like the werewolves and weretigers, preferring what nature gave them.

"I always knew you would come to me."

The sensual voice behind Kalina caused her heart to jump. She whirled around, clutching the sapphire to her chest.

Eral. The naked man was just as handsome as he had been when she saw him last. His ocean-blue eyes twinkled and she caught her breath as she looked at his long silvery-blond hair. His smile was sensuous as he caught her wrists in his and brought her hands to his chest. She understood what powerless meant as he drew her so close his rigid cock brushed her belly and his lips pressed against her forehead. She heard his deep inhale and he sighed as he said, "Your scent...like mint and sweet tea."

Kalina shivered. One of her palms was flat against his smooth-muscled chest, and her other hand clenched the sapphire tight between them. She could not help but drink in the musky scent of him, as he was doing with her. He smelled of the ocean, of all that was wild and free beneath its waters.

She knew she was here for another reason, but right now she could not think. She tilted her head up to look at him and he immediately took her mouth in one of his kisses that was like nothing she had ever experienced before meeting him.

His kiss was gentle, yet firm and commanding. She found herself leaning in closer, her nipples brushing his chest, and she grew wet between her thighs. All she could think about was him taking her down to the floor and driving his cock deep inside her. Images of the two of them together filled her mind…memories of her skin changing colors with her orgasms as he filled her with his seed.

Before she knew it she had her arms wrapped around his neck and his hands clenched her buttocks tight. His cock was so hard against her belly that she could imagine what it would feel like inside her.

She was lost…lost in the kiss. Lost in her desire for this man. Lost in her need to be with him.

But then the vision came to her sharp and sudden, a flash of pain behind her eyes and the heat of the stone in her hand.

Kalina pushed her free hand against his chest and shoved. Eral's expression was puzzled as he released her, yet still his blue gaze burned with fire. She almost flung herself against him, wrapped her legs around his waist and let him drive himself into her.

Almost.

Almost.

Shaking with the force of her need, she raised the apple-sized sapphire between the two of them and took a deep breath. "I'm here…" She swallowed. "I'm here to give you a warning. Your people are in danger — the king is in grave peril. I only hope I am not too late to stop what I have seen."

Chapter Four

ھ

In Kalina's open palms she held a blue sapphire. Its glassy depths pulsed as if the light trapped inside was echoing her warning. "I need to speak to King Lawl, immediately." Her voice was tight and insistent. A tremor shook her as she gripped the stone tightly.

Her words froze Eral for only a second, before he forced a smile and closed his hands around hers. An unexpected rush of heat radiating from the gem made him loosen his grip, and then he firmed it once again. "You did not brave the sea to be with me?" An uneasy laugh parted his lips. Yet, the alarm that flashed in her eyes spoke the truth. Disappointment warred with the sense of foreboding that slid across his flesh like a wrasse, quick and silent, raising the hairs on his arms.

Instead of releasing her, Eral pulled her to him again. He had to touch her, feel her body against his. The need he felt for this woman was unsettling. It was as though his hands had a mind of their own, as well as his cock that hardened when his fingers came into contact with her soft skin. "The King has left to meet with his betrothed. They are to be joined in a week's time."

Kalina went easily into his arms. Her body melted against his and he found himself supporting her, as if her knees had given out. "Then I am too late," she whispered.

Her reaction shocked him. She had always been so self-assured, so confident. Yet he felt her vulnerability and her sense of failure. Ice froze his heart.

Maintaining his hold on her so she would not fall, he held her at arm's length and gazed down upon her. "What is this danger that you believe is to befall my people?"

"A black cloud. Death. Many of your people." She paused, before continuing. "The king's death." She spoke with assurance leaving no doubt she believed what the stone revealed. Her skin was cool against his hands. He wondered whether the shiver he felt pass through her was from the trip below the waters or the vision she believed was to become reality.

"Cloud?" Eral tried to keep his voice light, hide the concern he felt rising like an imminent tidal wave. "We are below water, my little witch." He curled a strand of her hair around his finger and pulled, forcing her to look at him. Her beauty stole his breath. When he was able to speak again, he said, "There are no clouds." Relaxing the muscles in his face and body, he attempted to mask his true feelings, as his mind raced to find reason behind her vision.

With the change of weather or a quake in the earth, the ocean floor had been known to shift and rise to form a wall of sand, but he would not call it a black cloud. Even the sediments in the water would not create such a thing as Kalina described. Yes, it could be difficult to breathe—to see within a storm of sand and swirling water, but not mortal peril to a werefin or other sea life. Not to mention that Lawl was too intelligent to lead their people into danger.

Kalina stepped away from him and he released her shoulders. Determination hardened her features. "You doubt me?" Spots of color dotted her cheeks and her normally serene expression appeared as though she was hurt he had questioned her.

No. He knew too much about her abilities to doubt her prediction. Yet he struggled with the thought of the loss of life—his brother's death. Although Eral believed, he refused to accept her words. "A prophecy can be changed depending on the action taken, can it not?"

He reached for her, but she stepped back again as she nodded. Concern etched lines in her forehead. "Destiny is an inevitable succession of events. Be warned, my vision has spoken. Yet it is unknown if what I have seen has been set into motion. Just remember that the pendulum could swing in the opposite direction than what you seek."

As if every disc in his back came alive they rolled one at a time, his backbone stiffening as his chin rose. If he was deemed to change fate, so be it. "I shall stop this tragedy before it happens."

The people of Atlantis would live.

His brother would *not* die.

Using the mind-link his people possessed he called upon his younger brother and Klon. If only the connection worked as far away as Lawl was, he could warn his brother himself. But their people could link only so far before it was broken.

Godsdamn. Eral resisted the urge to curse aloud. He should be attending to this situation himself. He fought the impulse to release his werefin cry and yell in frustration to go after his brother himself. But above all else, it was his duty to remain behind — to protect the city of Atlantis and their people in the king's absence. A warrior first and foremost, Eral's need to protect his brother was strong. His fingers itched to hold his crossbow. The muscles in his arms tightened and then relaxed, pulsing with the desire to release his magic and wrath upon the unseen foe.

Within seconds Derel and Klon, both warriors of the Atlantis Marina, stood before Eral. The minute his younger brother saw Kalina he slid his blue gaze across the naked woman's body and grinned. The damn man even licked his lips as if in anticipation. Yes. It was true the brothers had shared women, but not this one. This one was Eral's.

Klon had more sense and bowed, keeping his eyes directed on Eral.

Klon's deference did nothing to reduce Eral's hot rush of jealousy. He growled at Derel. It was a primitive need to protect what belonged to him, this woman who had ensnared him completely. His low rumble received an expression of surprise from both Kalina and Derel. Then his younger brother's grin deepened with acknowledgement. The gleam in his eyes announced there would be hell to pay later in the way of teasing. But there was no time to think about such things. Not now, when Lawl's life and those of their people were at risk.

Eral gathered his resolve even though the responsibility he felt was like four walls closing slowly in on him. The air became thick as he forced a breath. "The sorceress has foreseen tragedy for our people—" his voice hardened, "and our king."

Derel's grin vanished as if it had never been. His posture went rigid. The gleam in his eyes disappeared. Instead, he stood erect, instantly the warrior he had been trained to be.

The fire that Eral felt deep within his soul burned in Derel's eyes. And for the first time in his brother's life, Derel bowed to Eral. The meaning sent a sharp pang to Eral's heart. "What is it you would have us do to prevent this prophecy, my Prince?"

Emotions bombarded Eral in all directions, pulling, pushing and swamping him all at once. This was not the way it was supposed to be.

I was never meant to rule.

With as much diplomacy as he could call forth, Eral reeled in his feelings and faced Kalina. "I need to know every detail of your vision."

Her amber eyes searched his face. The sorceress's continued silence was like fingernails across a smooth surface. He wanted to shake her—force the words from her mouth.

"Speak!"

She flinched at his outburst. Immediately his gaze softened toward Kalina. He had not meant to direct his apprehension at her.

The woman he had held close disappeared and the seer appeared. The controlled demeanor she held tightly set him further on edge. She raised her head, held out the sapphire as she peered into it. "The king and his entourage will encounter a cloud of black. If this is true, many will die, including your king."

"Is it the future you see or the past or present? How far away from the Kingdom of Incasha are they? How much time do we have?" Eral's questions came rapidly, one after the other as his gut clenched. Thoughts whirled in his mind. Lawl had only been gone half a day. How fast was he traveling? Had he taken any detours? If Derel left now it would take him at the very least a day to reach Lawl, warn him of the danger and then another day to return with news.

Kalina shook her head. "It is unknown to me."

Eral's fingers curled into fists. "Godsdamn!" he barked in frustration at her vagueness, then sharply pivoted to confront Derel. This time when he spoke it was brother to brother. "Lawl should be reaching Incasha by nightfall. Alert our guards and select a few trusted werefins to accompany you." He swallowed hard then reached for Derel and pulled him into a brotherly embrace. "Take care, little brother," he whispered against Derel's ear before releasing him. Eral turned to Klon. "Issue a warning that no one is to enter the water until I deem it safe."

There was no fear in Derel's eyes, only determination as he and Klon departed. Pride for his sibling fluttered in Eral's chest like the brush of wings, then that heavy weight rolled back in.

If danger lurked beyond the safe haven of Atlantis the last thing Eral wanted was to place Derel in danger, too. But he had no choice. Many of the warriors of the Atlantis Marina were skilled and trustworthy, but he trusted no one more than Derel with the king's—their brother's—life.

Once Derel left, Eral consulted with the three remaining heads of the Atlantis Marina forces. There were five in total—two were away in attendance with the king.

While Eral called upon the commanders, Kalina remained quietly by his side.

Monro was the eldest of the three men who arrived, and he bowed before Eral. The graying werefin's head rose. His keen eyes looked weighted with concern despite his normally sour expression. "You have beckoned us, Prince Eral?"

"I seek your assistance, milords." Ceham's and Nodic's eyes widened with Eral's request. They glanced at each other. These two men had never been supportive of Eral's carefree way of life, nor his choices. They were straightlaced warriors. Fun could not be found anywhere in their strict book of rules.

Eral gestured toward Kalina. "May I present Kalina, sorceress and seer to the Tarok kings."

A flicker of a frown passed over her features. She bowed deeply to each of the commanders. The men eyed her with raised eyebrows.

"The *former* sorceress of the Tarok kings," Eral corrected, before continuing. "She has delivered a warning that danger threatens Atlantis, as well as our king's life. I have sent Derel with a troop to intercept King Lawl. As for the safety of Atlantis, I ask your assistance in posting guards."

Monro's voice was like the rumblings of an earthquake. "I do not mean to offend, milady, but under whose authority do you bring this news?"

Kalina's shoulders squared. She held herself tall and proud. "I need no one's authority. My visions have spoken. I only wish to be of assistance."

Nodic smirked and turned his attention to Eral. "It is not your suggestion that we heed her words."

It was a statement rather than a question that Eral heard in the older man's tone. Eral's backbone went rigid.

A grin played at the corners of Nodic's mouth and Monro's expression turned even more sour than normal.

Eral's temper rose. He glared, and for the first time he could remember, unleashed the tone his father and brother used when issuing commands. "Post guards around Atlantis. Now. Ensure the guards are relieved regularly—no fatigue or wandering concentration. Make certain no post is left unattended, even for a moment. A scouting party is to be kept on patrol. I will not have Atlantis vulnerable in the king's absence."

The commanders stood straighter. Their smirks and glowers vanished. Looks of concern—mingled with a splash of respect—flowed over their faces.

With a nod, Eral added, "You will excuse us. And make haste. On a regular basis I want to be kept apprised of all oddities around and beyond our realms."

The men paused then bowed before leaving to attend to the duties Eral had given them. The expressions on their faces made it clear they did not believe Kalina's prediction, but at least they now knew they were obligated to follow Eral's instructions.

When they were alone, Eral turned back to Kalina and she bowed her head. "I have failed the King of Atlantis."

The cool demeanor she presented him with was disturbing. He had been too abrupt with her.

Eral took several steps to close the distance between them. With a swipe of his hand, he stroked her hair aside and she raised her gaze to meet his. He slid his palm to the back of her neck, bringing her closer to him. "You braved your fear of water to warn my brother of this impending danger." In no way would he forget he owed her a debt of gratitude. "It is not clear if anything has occurred. Until then we must wait."

"Yes, however—"

He placed a finger against her parted lips then replaced it with his mouth. She was soft and pliable beneath him, but her grip on his arm with her free hand said something different. He felt dread tremble through her as the kiss ended.

Damn. He couldn't allow her to remain in such a state. They had done what they could for the moment. Now she needed some distraction. He needed distraction, too.

His palm slid down her arm, capturing her hand in his. "Come, let me show you Atlantis."

Before he could lead her away, Kalina held up the sapphire, offering it to him. "For safekeeping," she said.

He took the stone from her and a strange tingle traveled over his palm. In the next moment it vanished from his hand. "I have sent it to our pelt vault for safekeeping," he said.

Kalina nodded. "Now that the sapphire is in the vault, I will be able to retrieve it and send it back at will."

Eral raised a brow. The fact that she had such power in his realm was surprising at the least.

He led her back toward the fountain aligned with enormous shells. Standing before the immortalized werefins of stone he said, "These are replicas of my father, grandfather, great-grandfather and grandfathers before them. They guard the entrance to the palace." Silently, he prayed that the magic ensconced within them and those of his people would be enough to fight the unknown enemy jeopardizing their paradise beneath the sea.

Kalina's hand was cool as she touched his arm. "Their life-force surrounds your city. It is strong—very strong magic."

Eral placed his hand over hers. A sense of pride filled him as he breathed deeply. "Our walls have never been penetrated." War was nearly unheard of below the surface of the water. Danger only shadowed them when they were aboveground.

As he thought of Kalina's words, he frowned. Perhaps this was the magic that Lawl attempted to speak to him about, important information Eral had casually brushed aside.

Anger rose suddenly, so hot he felt it consume him in a red ball of fury. "We will defeat this enemy."

Kalina's voice was soothing as she spoke. "There is greatness within you, Prince Eral." Her words began to calm the disquiet inside him, until she said, "You are a leader even though you struggle with your calling."

Was there nothing hidden from this woman? His fingers pushed through his hair. A man had to have his secrets. "Come, there is more to view." His people needed to see him walk among them and to know that whatever danger may lurk, he was there to protect them.

Holding hands, they strolled through the tall, enormous caverns, soft blue light glistened off the ceilings and walls. His people, naked as was normal for their world, walked about and attended to their duties and lives.

Eral squeezed Kalina's hand and looked at her. She was so beautiful that it nearly took his breath away. How easy it would be to lose himself in her. If it were not for the danger she foretold…

They needed a distraction. For now. "Tell me, my mystery woman, more about you. Let us start where we left off."

Her amber eyes stared straight ahead and she seemed to close off to him. The last time they had spent together she had been relaxed, perhaps more receptive to his questions. "I am a seer," she said. "I have served kings. I have served lords. What more matters?"

He stopped them by tugging her hand and bringing her to face him. Using his knuckles, he caressed her jawline. "Everything about you matters, Kalina."

For a moment she appeared to relax a little. She closed her eyes and leaned into his touch as he brushed his hand upward and pushed her hair behind her ear. When she opened her eyes, her expression of serenity was back in place. "I do believe you promised to show me more of Atlantis."

Even though he was disappointed, Eral gave a low bow of his shoulders. "This way, milady," he said before they continued their walk.

At the dock, children laughed as they switched between human and werefin forms. Their glossy pelts sparkled with innocence, little legs reappearing as they scrambled to their feet. Dynasty, their teacher, instructed them to send their pelts quickly into the pelt vault, a magical place for storage and safekeeping.

Guarding one's pelt was the first thing a werefin child was taught.

Eral shuddered with the thought of what would happen if a pelt fell into the wrong hands. If an enemy was to possess a werefin pelt, the werefin would be lost, a slave to his new master. Or worse yet, if the pelt was destroyed, the werefin would die.

Dynasty's voice was like bells tinkling as she laughed at a little boy stuck between worlds as he floundered upon the ground. One human leg hung from his pelt. His chin quivered, but the tremor quickly disappeared to be replaced by an impish grin as Dynasty waved his pelt to the vault. Her long silvery hair, much like Eral's, floated upon the air as she knelt before the child. She tapped him once on the nose. "Tenne, you must concentrate." She reclined so that she leaned on a single hip. Immediately her long legs disappeared, her gorgeous rainbow pelt in their place. Her large, nearly transparent tail rose in the air and then patted the stone floor before rising again. It was a magnificent display. She was beautiful.

Kalina cleared her throat, capturing his attention. "Atlantis? You were showing me your kingdom."

A smile rose on Eral's face. The slender blonde had been a favorite of his until now. The dark beauty at his side stirred his loins like no other woman. If not for the churning in his gut at her prophecy, he would take her down and explore the mysteries of her body.

"Prince Eral." When his gaze rose it was to see the classroom of werefin children bowing low. He could not help but smile. They were a rowdy bunch. They twitched and squirmed in their positions of respect, obviously itching to be set free.

Through feathered lashes Dynasty peered at Eral. "The children wish to know if their prince would join them for a swim?" Her tail rose high and fell softly before her legs reappeared. She held her pelt in her graceful hands, then sent it back to the vault. She rose to stand on her long, slender legs and approached Eral and Kalina.

"Not today—" Eral started.

Immediately the children bombarded him with cries of "Puleeezeee".

If not for the danger threatening his city, he would have chuckled. He had swum and played frequently with the children of Atlantis upon his visits home from Lord Kir's Emerald City. The lighthearted laughter of children reminded him of his own childhood, of days spent frolicking about the sea.

Yet now the fates of his brother and Atlantis were in his hands.

In a flash the children were on their feet and surrounded him and Kalina.

It tore him up inside to look at their innocence, to know that their fates rested in his hands. "Not today, little tadpoles." He had to find some way to resolve the impending danger.

"Puleeezeee," they insisted.

His little witch looked taken back when a young girl grabbed her hand. "Will you swim with me?" the little redhead asked.

What appeared to be fear and then shame flashed across Kalina's face. She remained silent as Jewel continued to chatter her insistence.

Eral ruffled Tenne's hair. The dark-haired boy stood before him jumping up and down. Tenne would not stop until he got his way. Eral felt abashed, the boy was just like him. How had his father, much less Lawl, put up with him?

Tenne giggled as Eral saved Kalina by grabbing Jewel and swinging her up high into the air, causing her to squeal in delight. "Not today, little one." He set the child back on her feet. He needed to speak to Dynasty without the children present. "Who is the fastest?"

"I am. I am," each child yelled.

"Prove it. Race to the fathers' fountain, tag it and then run back to me. Now go," Eral shouted. As they raced off he turned to Dynasty. "Keep the children out of the water. It is only a precaution. I do not wish to scare our people, especially the children."

He knew the increase of guards and his order that no werefins enter the water would cause suspicion and anxiety. He just hoped that the people of Atlantis seeing him behave normally would reduce their fear and put them at ease.

He had other plans for Kalina. She would not be happy to be kept below the sea for so long, but at least she would be safe. A little charm and finesse and he should be able to distract her enough to accomplish what he needed to do to protect her.

"We have already received your orders to remain aground, *my* Prince." Dynasty's gaze skimmed over Kalina. "Does that also include the spawning beds? Rumor has it that you have an appointment. I thought perhaps of joining you." The seduction in the woman's voice would normally make his cock harden...but with Kalina at his side, no other woman interested him.

Just then a choir of female voices rose in the air. The magical sound beckoned him. There was nothing more enchanting as the song of his people. It was a delicate blend of soft music, beautiful words and mesmerizing magic drifting upon a summer breeze.

Godsdamn, Lawl. His brother had made an appointment for Eral to partake in the spawning, a mating ritual werefins used to find a partner. Two weeks ago he had agreed to appease Lawl, but that was before Eral discovered Kalina was his true mate. The six beautiful and sexy werefins awaiting him held no appeal. Instead, getting Kalina somewhere private was more to his liking—after he knew for certain his brothers were safe.

His chin rose, his lips parted and in the same melodic tone he responded to the women awaiting him, extending to them his deepest apologies. Sorrowful cries joined in with children's laughter as the brood returned out of breath. Fortunately, the children would not understand the meaning of the sensual song until they were of joining age.

Jumping up and down, Tenne laughed, "I won. I won. What is my prize, Prince Eral?"

Eral's fingers brushed the air and a shell appeared within his palm. He handed it to the boy.

Tenne's smile faded. "It is a shell."

"Ah, but did you examine it closely?" Eral asked, holding back a smile.

When Tenne peered into the small opening a gush of water sprayed him in the face. Stunned, the boy blinked and sputtered as all the children burst into laughter. Then a mischievous grin slid across Tenne's face. "Come, let us play a trick on Dalmont." Dalmont was another of the children's teachers, one not nearly as adored as Dynasty.

As they ran away, Dynasty said, "That was very naughty of you, Prince Eral." She reached out and squeezed his arm. "I will see you later." The woman's bare hips swayed as she walked away. She stopped briefly to glance over her shoulder and wink before continuing.

When Eral turned back to Kalina her face was flushed, her eyes narrowed, her expression far from her natural serenity. Surely, the woman was not jealous. The idea that she might actually care for him beyond just the physical gratification of sex sent a warm sensation straight to his cock and sent his mind into a chaotic frenzy. Now was not the time to be thinking of sex. One brother could already be in danger, the other heading straight for it.

And Eral was responsible for their people and Atlantis.

Wind tore at the King of Malachad's flowing white robe and separated the opening to expose his nakedness beneath. Balin's dark, long hair whipped across his face, the sting ignored as he stood on the rocky beach and glared across the foamy sea. Whitecaps crashed into the surf and then savagely pulled it back into its embrace. The angry clouds above mimicked the fire rolling and churning in his stomach.

His plans to overtake Emerald City had been destroyed by Prince Eral. Balin had not only had Abby, but Lord Kir within his grasp. But the werefin had interfered, saving them both.

Never again. He raised his head and roared. The cry of rage rose upon the breeze carrying it across water and land. No. Never again would the fish-man walk the earth or for that matter swim the ocean.

Balin's fists clenched as he inhaled a mouthful of salty air. The brine mixed with a strong odor of fish was a reminder why he stood on the beach this afternoon. In his fury, his talons sharpened, biting into his skin. He turned to face his army of *bakirs*. They had failed him time and again. Actually they had been Mikaela's men and women who possessed physic powers and the ability to shapeshift into weretigers, just as she could. But his *dear* wife, the sister to the Tarok kings, had broken Balin's spell over her. She had fled when she discovered that she was responsible for raining terror upon the people of Tarok as well as her brothers—the four kings of Tarok—and her actions had almost killed their mates.

Now the ungrateful bitch roamed the lands with Kalina, the sorceress who had assisted her. He rolled his shoulders, trying to release the tension gripping him. No matter how many scouting parties he sent out time and time again, their whereabouts were still unknown. Just the thought of Mikaela's treacherous behavior, the fact that she had left him, turned his blood hot with rage. Both Mikaela and Kalina would pay when he had both of them under his control. For now his sights were set on Atlantis and ridding this world of werefins altogether.

One particular woman in the army of *bakirs* behind him stood out, beautiful and supple. When he'd turned to face the army, the sorceress raised her brown eyes to meet his—without his permission. She was bold. Perhaps too bold. Letta had proven to not only have physic powers, but he discovered that she was a strong sorceress as well. Surprisingly, he could trace her lines back to a family of sorcerers he had thought extinct from a realm too far for him to conquer.

The woman held a desire for power that stirred Balin. It both excited and angered him. He needed to control her—break her.

All the *bakirs* were dressed in black robes. Yet, she wore a red silk robe. He had taken her from their fighting lines into his palace. She had proven to be great sport both in bed and on the torturing racks.

With a mere nod, he called her to him.

She came willingly and bowed before him as her thick, wavy brunette hair spilled over her shoulders. "Sire." Looking up at him through her lashes, she enticed him with a coy expression he knew was only a ploy. Still his cock jerked alive. A gust of wind blew open his robe again to display his thickness.

Godsdamn but he wanted her. Right now. But the knowing smile on her face made him want to punish her before their task, before they began the process that would destroy Atlantis and Prince Eral.

He knew he should deprive Letta, but then he would be depriving himself and he would not allow that to happen. "Take off your robe."

Her movements were slow and sensuous as she unfastened the sash, slipped it from around her waist and let the breeze carry it away. Balin watched as the strip of red cloth dipped, rose and then dipped again before wrapping itself around a blue feather-leaved *ch'tok* tree. Through the slit in her robe he could see her cleavage, the swells of her breasts, and her shaved mons. With a simple shrug the silk slipped from her arms, the wind catching it to whisk it a distance away to land on the beach. She stood proudly, her warrior training apparent as his gaze stroked every curve of her body.

Soon her full lips would part and take him deep. He would fuck her mouth and she would enjoy it. That fact annoyed him. His pleasure was the only thing that mattered. He reached out and with both hands cupped her breasts so that his talons pierced her tender skin. Through clenched teeth that showed when she winced, she inhaled a strained breath. A teardrop of blood formed around each talon as he pushed them a little farther into her flesh.

Moisture filled her eyes, but he could tell by the upward angle of her chin, she refused to let one tear fall. He released his pressure, allowing sensation to flow back into her breasts, knowing the pain would intensify. Deliberately, he dragged his nails across the pale globes to her nipples, enjoying the red angry path his fingernails left behind.

Her eyes lowered and focused on his cock as she kept control over her pain. There was nothing like a woman's scream. This one had been trained too well in accepting agony. He knew he wouldn't hear a sound out of her. Even when he grabbed her nipples and twisted, she remained silent.

Then her eyes rose to meet his. When she ran her finger through the blood seeping from her wounds then slipped it into her mouth and sighed, Balin jerked her to him.

He ravaged her mouth, stealing her breath as he thrust his tongue hard and fast. He especially enjoyed the point where she gagged as he pushed his tongue deep. Then he bit her lip, drawing blood. It was sweet on his tongue as he pushed her away from him.

"On your knees," Balin demanded, releasing the sash around his waist. He grasped himself in one hand, while the other grabbed a handful of Letta's hair as her knees sank into the sand. With a snap he jerked her head back so the delicate line of her neck was stressed to its limits. The surprised cry she released made him smile. Her eyes widened and for a moment he thought he saw fear. He liked fear. Instead her eyes began to grow smoky with desire.

Godsdamn. She reminded him of Mikaela. Nothing frightened that woman but herself. He had not been able to break his wife, but he would tame this woman.

"Bring me my crystal ball," he commanded to a *bakir* as he began to stroke himself gently, teasing Letta by rubbing the crown of his cock across her lips. She flicked her tongue across the small slit.

From the crowd, a *bakir* approached. In his hands he held Balin's most trusted visionary tool. Balin released his cock and took the clear quartz into his palms, the *bakir* remaining by his side. Even beneath the sea the werefin could not escape him. All Balin needed was a weak mind to filter his magic through. The land was filled with weaklings like John Steele. Balin looked past his congregation to where the cage sat. The human man was scrunched in the small confinement. He had escaped Balin before, but he would not again.

Steele had once been mated with the King of Clubs' Queen, Awai. Apparently the woman had not enjoyed a life of servitude and punishment at Steele's hands. Just as Steele had not when Balin turned the tables and placed him in that role. The human had been amusement for a while, but his escape had infuriated Balin. It was time to make good use of this troublesome man.

71

But for now he needed to see what the werefins were up to. He stared down upon Letta. When he fucked her or she sucked his cock, she had made his visions stronger—clearer. Never before had he been able to see beneath the waves. And the irony of it all was that the sorceress had no idea that each time they fucked he consumed a little of her magic. He felt her powers growing inside him. Before he was through with Letta he would own her body and soul.

"Take me into your mouth." As he thrust his hips forward, burying his cock between Letta's lips, he thrust the crystal ball toward the sky. The woman's mouth was wet and tight as she sucked, her head bobbing in a slow rhythm. Every once in a while he felt her teeth scrape him, while her tongue swirled around the rim of his crown.

Eyes pinned on the crystal, Balin watched as it began to glow and a vision of King Lawl appeared. The leader was traveling east, nearing Incasha, with an entourage of his people.

Balin smiled as his future vision showed him what would soon happen. An enormous beast would release a poisonous cloud that would spare no one—nothing. A beast created by his and Letta's hands. Hands that now fondled his sac, squeezing his balls until they ached.

With King Lawl away from Atlantis, that would mean Prince Eral was indeed down in what would become his grave. Werefins were so predictable.

Balin used his mind-scan to search the water for Atlantis. The palace materialized within the crystal ball. Many werefins were going about performing their daily rituals. The smaller of the breed were practicing changing from werefin to human and back again.

Letta moaned around Balin's cock and he felt the vibration race through him causing him to lose his hold on the vision. When his eyes refocused his body went rigid.

Beside Prince Eral—that woman.

The sorceress Kalina.

Anger like he had never felt before surged like a hot iron through him. Had the sorceress warned the werefin? Another rush of fury caused his orgasm to rip from him and his seed to shoot down Letta's throat. His hips thrust forward and a cry burst from his lips as he clutched the crystal in his hands still high above his head.

When the pulse in his groin died and his mind calmed, he lowered the crystal and handed it back to the *bakir* who waited patiently beside him.

Balin slipped from Letta's mouth, closed his robe and quickly tied his sash. "It is time," he announced. "Bring Steele to me." Then he gazed down upon Letta. "Rise and prepare the potion."

"Motherfuckers," Steele growled and then groaned in pain as two *bakirs* dragged him out of his cage. He shivered as his muscles attempted to stretch, unable to stand to his normal height of over six feet.

Balin almost vomited from the stench of the man. For a week now, Steele had been confined in the cage where he could do no more than sit or hunch over, wallowing in his own excrement.

Balin growled, "Hurry with the potion." Then he turned and faced Steele again. "It is time for you to do my bidding."

"Go fuck yourself," Steele said with a wildness in his eyes that bordered on insanity.

Balin chuckled. "Why should I when I have you?" He would fuck the man if the bastard was not so repulsive. As Letta approached, Balin said, "Hold Steele down."

Steele snapped. He struggled so ferociously on the rocky beach that even in his weakened condition it took three *bakirs* to hold him and another to pry his mouth open. Letta drained the potion down his throat.

When he was released, the change was almost immediate. Steele sputtered and coughed as he curled into a ball in obvious agony. Grasping his legs to his chest he rolled upon the sandy ground. Like a pulsing organ his head began to swell then collapse, swell then collapse. Each time it left the upper portion of his head larger, as if his brain was growing, bigger and bigger. Eyes bulging, his jaws lengthened and came together like a parrot's bill. Then his arms and legs split in two and elongated, while the bones in his abdomen and chest shrunk to a web of tissue that joined his arms and legs to his body at the base. Fingers and toes melted together and in their stead were tentacles—eight of them aligned with suction cups on the inside of each extremity.

John Steele had been transformed into an octopus.

He was enormous, measuring close to twenty-eight feet from the tip of one arm to the tip of another on the opposite side of his body. His arms were as thick as three men. His head was as large around as a castle turret, and twice the height of Balin.

The stress the former man was under made its pigment bags connect with its nervous system as it began to change from a gray color to the eggshell color of the sand beneath him. It was a natural survival mechanism to blend into his environment. Yet it was fear that made his skin change from red to purple, blue to yellow, until finally it was brown with red stripes.

The beast's large head draped to one side as its long arms slithered across the sand, pulling it closer and closer to the water's edge. As the waves crashed against it, the octopus slowly began to submerge, sucking in water and squeezing it through its siphon, a funnel-shaped opening under its head that moved it backward and deeper into the depths, until it was no longer visible.

Balin traced a single finger over one of the hieroglyphics tattooed on his cheekbones, the sign of infinity—a figure eight lying sideways that had a bold line above the symbol. "Fascinating. Are you positive the poison within Steele will work?"

Letta moved beside him. "Most assuredly." He saw the amusement in her eyes. She clapped her hands and the army of *bakirs* stepped aside.

Every muscle tightened in his body with anticipation of the havoc that would reign below its blue-green surface. "Steele will do my bidding?"

"Yes, Sire." Letta leaned closer so that he could feel her breath brush the side of his cheek. "The human—or should I say, octopus—will do as you command. It knows its death will not be quick or painless if it does not obey you." Her hand slipped beneath the sleeve of Balin's robe. Her fingers were warm as she stroked his arm.

He glanced down at the brunette, her nipples taut and her blood-streaked breasts heavy with need. She deserved a reward. He slipped his fingers through her silky brown hair, before grasping her tightly at the nape of her neck. He pulled her close, so that their lips were a breath apart. "Perhaps I will fuck you all night long."

Her chest rose with each inhale. "As you wish, my King."

He yanked her roughly against his chest. The last thing Balin remembered as he took the woman down to the sand was that tonight Prince Eral and all his people would be destroyed. The werefin would not interfere again.

Chapter Six

ഇ

Kalina stood beside Eral in the King's chamber of the palace. It was a bright room filled with color from coral and shells, rich with treasures from the sea. But she barely noticed the room. She felt Eral's fear for his brothers to her very bones. It was obvious in the tightening of his jaw and the rigidness in his posture. Constant cool air circulated in the palace, keeping the rooms from becoming stagnant. The air brushed her bare skin, but she had become used to it and goose bumps no longer prickled her flesh whenever there was a fresh breeze caressing her skin.

Derel had been gone for two days, and Kalina grew nearly as restless and concerned as Eral. Their sex the past night had been desperate, fast and furious. He had taken her again and again, spending his frustration within her. If she had not collapsed from exhaustion and told him she could take no more, she was certain he would have fucked her all night.

With every orgasm her magic had threatened to come to the surface and it had become harder and harder to push it away. The last orgasm had almost been too much. She had nearly been in tears from the power it had taken to shove that magic too far back to surface.

Could she keep a tight leash on it much longer?

"My brother should have returned by now." Eral's words had a raw and angry edge to them. He slammed his fist against the closest thing to him, a wall of fine coral. His hand rammed through the lacy but rock-hard wall. When he yanked his fist out, he was bleeding from multiple cuts. Kalina would have gone to him, but she sensed his need to feel physical pain. The fact that he felt so helpless while his brothers were in danger was obvious in his every move, his every word. "Gods, I need to do *something!*"

"I will try the stone again," Kalina said in a firm voice that belied her concern.

Eral whirled on Kalina, fire in his eyes. "It has been useless since you brought it."

Knowing that Eral was merely venting his frustration, Kalina said nothing as he watched her. She called the sapphire from the pelt vault where she had sent it for safekeeping after each attempt to find answers within its depths. Her own frustration had mounted as the stone had told her nothing since she had arrived in Atlantis.

When the large, round stone appeared in her hand, this time a strong feeling rocked her, one she had never experienced before. At first she rebelled against it—she always obtained her visions alone. But now it was telling her that she needed Eral's strength as well as her own.

She took a deep breath and her eyes met Eral's fiery blue gaze. "Hold the stone with me." She raised the sapphire with both hands. "It is telling me I cannot see the future without you."

For a moment he paused, his jaw tense and a vein pulsing along his neck. The muscles in his chest and biceps flexed as he raised his arms. The moment his hands clasped over hers and the stone, a burst of energy shot through Kalina, so powerful she stumbled back. Only Eral's hold on her hands kept her from falling.

Even as images started flashing before her eyes, she saw shock in Eral's expression.

Kalina closed her eyes and tried to focus on the vision, tried to slow the images down so that she could understand what was happening—and what had happened.

A proud male werefin surrounded by an entourage of werefin guards gracefully swam through the water, their pelts shimmering with every movement. Her senses told her immediately that the lead werefin was King Lawl. The men and women warriors along with the king carried bows, and quivers of arrows were slung over their backs.

Incasha. The name came easily to her mind as they neared a city. Eral had told her the city's name and the stone confirmed it. The city was domed, the surface clear as the water surrounding it. If she had not been told of its existence she would have missed the faint shimmer of its walls. Within the city she saw werefin men, women and children walking, working, playing in their human, naked forms. There was air within the city and the dome held the water out so that the werefin could live in both worlds — as humans or werefins.

Kalina's heart pounded, the thump crawling up to lodge in her throat. The powerful feeling of wrongness was so strong she wanted to scream at the king to flee. She wanted to scream at the people she saw going so casually about their business. Somehow their home would become a death trap.

A crystal-clear entrance suddenly appeared. Doors opened, barely visible as they sparkled in the water. The doors were tall and wide, and Lawl and his entourage entered.

Ice coated Kalina's body as an enormous beast rounded an outcropping of rock and shot toward the city. *Octopus*, the stone told her. It was an abnormally large octopus and her seer's senses told her it carried within it a black cloud of death.

She held back another scream and clenched her eyes and her teeth tighter.

Before the doors closed, the beast reached the dome and immediately clamped on to the clear surface with huge suckers on its massive arms. It swung its upper body so that it was inside the domed city.

Lawl and his warriors whirled and drew their bows. With lightning-fast speed, they started firing at the beast.

It was too late.

Black ink spewed from a sac near the belly of the abnormal beast. The substance was not the normal ink an octopus used for protection. No, this was poison, a cloud of death.

Kalina's hands shook. She felt Eral's hands that were as ice-cold as hers, and knew he watched the vision with her.

The moment the cloud encompassed the entourage, they dropped their weapons and grabbed their throats.

At the same moment his warriors had drawn their bows, Lawl raised his hands and gave a magical cry of his people. A glow surrounded him—a type of shield. But a shield that had not been thrown up fast enough for some of the black cloud to slide by.

Ancestral magic, came to Kalina's mind. *The shield—it is magic inherited from his forefathers.*

Gold streams of the ancestral magic ripped from his fingers like lightning and struck the belly of the beast. Again and again the bolts blasted the beast. And again he gave the powerful magical cry.

But Lawl's magic began to weaken. The black cloud that had slid by was invading his system.

Lawl's shield vanished. He dropped to his knees and swayed. He raised his hands as if to release further magic, then pitched forward, facedown, to lie as still as the other werefins around him.

The beast's cry of pain from the magic reverberated through the domed space but the black cloud was already spreading in the air across the city with the speed of a weretiger after its prey.

Eral's hands were clenching Kalina's so tight the stone dug into her palms.

She watched in horror as people within the city were screaming, running...and then dropping, dying. There was no place the vapor did not reach. It crept into homes, places of business, schools, play areas. Nothing was untouched. No one escaped death.

Just as Kalina was going to open her eyes, her vision was transported outside the clouded walls of the domed city. To her increasing horror she saw Derel and the werefins he had taken with him. The octopus was pushing away from the dome, the pain in its belly from the magic obvious. The cloud followed behind it as it fled. One of its arms slammed into Derel who was flung up against a wall covered in the same type of yellow sea sponges that Eral had used during their bath.

The warriors who had been with Derel dropped to the ocean floor, including Klon. The ink encompassed Derel, too. He started to push away from the sponges then brought his hand to his throat. He clutched one of the sponges apparently to keep from falling. He held on to it as the ink was sucked back into the domed city. The doors slammed behind it, holding the black cloud within its once clear walls.

From a distance Kalina heard a loud cry. She jerked herself out of the vision. Her eyes snapped open and she realized she was screaming. Eral howled his rage, too.

He released the stone and her hands, grabbed her by her upper arms and shook her so hard it made her dizzy and she almost dropped the sapphire. If she did not know that he was so angry at what had happened to his brothers, she would have been upset at his treatment of her. But she knew he was venting the feelings the vision had given him.

"Tell me," he said through clenched teeth as he stopped shaking her. "Is this a future vision? Tell me it is so that I might stop it."

"Past." She swallowed, the knowledge sliding through her veins from the stone like ice water. "It has already happened."

Eral's grip on her tightened so hard he was bruising her arms. The expression on his face changed from fury to pain and back to fury.

He released her and thrust her away from him hard enough to cause her to stumble back. His expression was so tortured, so filled with pain that she wished she could go to him, comfort him.

Eral clenched his fists at his sides. "Tell me what more you see in the stone—"

"Your Highness!"

A shout caused Eral and Kalina to whirl to the entrance to the throne room. Through the doors two men supported Derel as his feet barely moved one after another. His features were gray, deathlike, and in one hand he clutched a yellow sea sponge.

Eral immediately strode toward the men and caught Derel in his arms. He held his brother tight as the men stepped away. "Thank the gods you are alive, Derel." Kalina heard tears in Eral's voice as he spoke. He leaned far enough back that he could see Derel's face. "Lawl?"

Derel's features paled beneath the gray of his skin. "Dead." His voice was a rusty croak. "Everyone but me. Dead. Even Klon." The pain in his voice ripped Kalina's heart apart.

Eral gripped his brother in his embrace, holding Derel up as he buried his face in his brother's hair.

The yellow sea sponge caught Kalina's eye. She moved forward and squeezed Derel's palm around the sponge with her hands. She remembered the way it had made her feel during the bath—as if it held some kind of healing powers. "The sponge. It spared your life?"

Eral drew back again and Derel gave a single nod. "I believe it is so." He pushed back from Eral, but Eral still held his brother by his shoulders. Derel swayed to and fro but did not fall. "As long as I held the sponge I had strength. I could breathe. I had life."

"He must be taken to the healer at once." Eral eyed the two men who still waited in the chamber.

"Yes, Your Majesty," they said as one, and proceeded to help Derel walk toward the healer's chambers.

"*Your Majesty*," Eral ground out after the men left. "I cannot be king. There has been a mistake. Lawl must still be alive—he was meant to rule, not me."

Kalina heard more than denial at his brother's death in Eral's voice. She sensed his fear of ruling the city of Atlantis, of not living up to expectations. But most of all she sensed and felt his pain at the loss of his brother and his people.

Eral raked his fingers through his long silvery-blond hair. "He cannot be dead. He cannot."

"You are now King of Atlantis." Kalina's hands tightened on the sapphire. "The stone is telling me you must lead your people to safety." Eral made a growling sound as he narrowed his gaze at her. "This city is no longer safe," she continued. "As soon as the beast discovers Atlantis' location, he will attack with the black cloud."

Eral just stared at her for a long moment. Kalina watched him steadily, her chin high as she looked at him with certainty.

A transformation came over Eral. Slight at first, then stronger. He straightened to his full height. His shoulders squared and appeared broader, his stance more kingly than the prince he had been. She no longer saw the teasing light in his eyes. In his gaze and expression she saw the weight of duty, responsibility and the power necessary to lead his subjects.

"I know of a place with many of the sea sponges," he said in a controlled voice. "Thousands. I will take my people there."

Kalina bowed before returning her gaze to his. "I will help in any way possible, Your Majesty."

Eral clenched his jaw as he reached out and caught her by her shoulders. For a moment she thought he might shake her again. Instead, he said, "To you I am Eral. Do not refer to me in any other manner. *Do you understand?*"

82

"In front of your subjects I must be respectful." She moved closer to him and wrapped her arms around his waist and pressed her face to his chest, trying to comfort him. "Eral, you are now king and you must be treated thusly by all."

Eral held her tight in his embrace. "I was not meant to rule."

Kalina raised her head. She clenched the sapphire in one fist and brought her free hand to his cheek and cupped it. "It is your destiny."

He released her. "Destiny or not, I must now inform my mother of Lawl's death." He took one step and paused, before pinching the bridge of his nose. His chest rose as he took a deep breath then headed toward his mother's chambers in the palace. Kalina did not follow. This was a time for family. A time for mourning the loss of a son, a brother and a king.

Despite the Atlanteans' attempt at maintaining a sense of calm, Kalina was almost overwhelmed by the tension in the air. It had taken mere hours for the werefins to prepare to leave their homes. One after another, the werefins transformed after sliding into the ocean and swimming in groups that Eral called "schools". The adults helped the children swim in the middle of the school, and some clutched baby werefins to their chests.

Kalina rubbed her arms as she watched. Her heart pounded as her terror rose. She wanted to go back home, to be free of the ocean and to once again run through trees and grass as a tiger, away from the water. But the stone told her that her task was not finished. She had to see this through.

And Eral. By the gods but something about him called to her like no other man ever had. It felt like a flock of *eloin* fluttered in her belly. The thought of leaving him hurt worse than the thought of returning home through the water.

Derel was nearly as strong as before, the sponge somehow slowly healing him.

A touch and then a clamping feeling on her wrist brought Kalina around to find herself facing Eral. His features were stern. He grasped her hand and brought it up so that she could see that an intricately designed band was now clasped around her wrist.

"What is this?" she said as his touch warmed her skin.

"It will allow you to breathe in the water." He maintained his hold on her as her eyes widened and she tried to take a step back. She bumped into one of the warriors surrounding them. The king's guard. "Its power is strong and will take oxygen from the water that you will take into your lungs and you will be able to swim underwater as the werefin do."

"No." Kalina violently shook her head as her heart pounded against her breastbone. "I will not. I refuse to go into the water." She gestured toward the dock. "The transport bubbles. I can go in one of those."

Eral held her gaze. "They are too slow. I will not put any of my people in danger by leaving them with such a burden."

"Then I will stay here." She clenched her hands into fists. "I am a weretiger, and I do not belong in the water. I cannot swim."

His intense blue gaze bored into hers. "You have no choice."

Kalina gritted her teeth. She started to tell him where to put his damned bracelet when he scooped her up in his arms and started walking toward the water's edge.

Absolute fear overcame her. She clawed at Eral's chest and struggled to free herself from his hold. Her movements became more frantic and she started to begin her transformation into a weretiger.

Before she could, Eral threw her into the water.

Kalina screamed as she hit the water. She sank below its surface and even then she screamed. Air came from her mouth in harsh bubbles and she tried to claw her way up to the surface. Fiery pain sliced behind her ears and she felt as if her flesh was opening.

She was sinking, sinking, running out of air. She held her breath until black spots danced before her eyes.

Everything went black.

Kalina woke in Eral's arms, wanting to vomit but unable to. In her confused state it took her a moment to realize her lungs were filled with water and she was actually breathing.

Yet again she panicked, trying to claw her way from Eral and holding her breath.

Calm yourself, Eral said in her mind as he embraced her. Mind-speech was universal between the weretigers and werewolves, as it was with the werefins. *Just breathe the sea in and out. The bracelet has given you gills, like mine.* He turned his head just enough that she saw small slits behind his ear that she had never noticed before. *They only appear when we are in the water,* he said.

She tried to control her racing thoughts, tried to lessen the fear that made knots in her belly. There was no fighting it now. It took all her effort to force herself to breathe in the water again.

Surprise filtered through her as she felt the cool rush of water in and out of her lungs and the oxygen that freely flowed through her body. *A gill is not all that different from a lung,* Eral again spoke in her mind. *Gills bind the oxygen and carry it to the tissues of your body.*

Kalina became aware of what was around her as she gradually accepted what was happening to her. Eral was in his werefin form. He was carrying her as he swam through sea life, past schools of fish, around growths that looked like flowers, and beside a sharp wall of coral. Eral pointed out bright yellow sea lilies, spiny-skinned animals and feather stars that waved their arms up and down as they moved through the water.

Around Eral and Kalina swam the king's guard. Despite the fact she was underwater, her senses were as sharp as ever—and she sensed that Eral was none too pleased at having an entourage surrounding him, protecting him. Yet he apparently had surrendered to the fact that as king he must be guarded at all costs.

With her acceptance of her place in this watery world, she "breathed" easier and saw the beauty of the werefins around her. Eral's tail looked almost silvery as it glimmered in the water. It was more silver than iridescent like the other werefins around them. Their fins sprouted from their backs and obviously helped to guide them through the water.

Eral had released her body and now only gripped her hand tightly as he led her through the obstacle course of scenery. Like on land, the ocean floor consisted of huge mountain ranges, broad basins and plains. He explained through their mind-link about places where there were long narrow valleys created by deep-sea sediments from land erosion and sea life. Add to that the colorful fish, anemones, plants and archways of coral and rock he pointed out, it was as if she had slipped into another world. She felt the gills behind her ears move ever so slightly and could not help but marvel at the magic of the band around her wrist.

Kick your legs, Eral instructed her. *It will enable us to move faster.*

Kalina obeyed, her legs stiff as tree trunks.

She heard Eral's laugh in her mind. *No, my little witch. Relax your legs.* He proceeded to give her instructions on how to swim and she finally understood enough that their travel went faster. A little. Of course Eral swam easily in his werefin form, but held back for her.

All the time they worked their way to the nest of sea sponges, Kalina felt on edge, like there was something in the recesses of her mind that would not quite let her rest. Not to mention the nagging unease of being beneath the water, having it fill her lungs.

To Kalina's relief they finally reached the bed of sea sponges that stretched for miles, yet surely Eral did not expect his people to be so exposed and out in the open. Then he veered to the left toward what appeared to be an enormous willowy tree growing from the side of a massive rock structure. With a brush of his hand he parted the seaweed branches to display the opening of a cave. As she peered inside she was taken aback by its beauty. It was more than she had imagined—a whole city could be built here. She saw werefin men, women and children going about tasks to set up their new home. Whether it be temporary or permanent, no one knew.

Eral held up at the entrance to the vivid yellow sea of sponges until all his people had entered. His guard surrounded him faithfully. Finally Eral motioned for them to remain where they waited for him. She sensed them arguing through their mind-links, but finally the guard remained where they had been as Eral slipped with Kalina around a corner and out of their sight and beyond the seaweed curtain. He held her tightly to him, her head resting against his shoulder, as if he was frightened he might lose her.

Warmth crept through Kalina and she experienced a headiness that she had never felt before. His lower body was still covered with his pelt and he felt warm and sensual against her.

She had never known confusion until she met Eral. Before him, she had felt definite in her choices and in the guidance of her seer's powers. But now...she did not know what to think any longer. She could only feel, and for some reason what she wanted to feel was more from Eral than she had ever expected of anyone. More than she had ever planned to ask of anyone.

Kalina would never love. Not in the way a woman loves a true mate. She had shared pleasures with many lovers throughout her century of life and there were many men she cared deeply for. But she had never felt love beyond friendship and closeness. She knew it must be the same now—she was meant to pleasure and be pleasured, and to aid others with her seer's abilities. Deep within her soul she had always believed this to be true.

Why then did she feel this way—different—as if Eral meant more to her somehow?

Come, my little witch, Eral spoke in her mind. *Even though they are around the corner, the guard fears for my safety.*

He leaned forward and pressed his mouth to hers, giving her a hard, fierce kiss. She opened enough to let him thrust his tongue in, and she wondered at the feel of water and his tongue in her mouth.

Just as he drew back and smiled, a shadow passed over them.

Kalina's heart pounded so hard her chest ached.

Terror ripped through her body as she saw what it was.

Chapter Seven

ɛɔ

The sudden fear on Kalina's face made Eral release her. In a swift movement he whipped his crossbow from where it was strapped behind his shoulder. Arrow instantly nocked into the bow, he spun and aimed at the looming shadow. Then his arms locked. The sudden strain vibrated up his arms.

Relief rushed through him and he lowered his crossbow.

Before him floated an enormous sea dragon. The animal flailed his small wings, moving quickly backward out of the deadly arrow's path. His spiny tail slid across the ocean floor, stirring sand in the water, and his pointed ears flattened against his head. His size and the abrupt movement sent a surge of water against Eral and Kalina causing white sand to swirl around them.

Eral's heart beat in his throat as he recognized the creature he had almost killed. Slowly, he lowered his bow.

Golgee! The animal's scratchy voice boomed in surprise, not to mention trepidation. *Is this how you greet a friend?* Air bubbles trickled from the dragon's flaring nostrils as he breathed rapidly. From the corner of Eral's eye he saw his guards had advanced, their arrows trained on the dragon as well.

Lacos. Relief gushed from Eral's mouth in a single breath. He brushed his hand through the water telling his men to lower their weapons. He shared the mind-link between him and the sea dragon with Kalina. Then he grasped her hand and squeezed. *It is only Lacos, my friend.* Lacos had the amazing ability to speak in all languages, animal or human. Eral wondered briefly what other traits this strange creature had that Eral may be unaware of.

Kalina's throat worked as she swallowed hard. *I thought...* Fear eased from her pale face as her gaze scanned the twenty-six-foot dragon bobbing with the ocean current. From the scaly tip of his tail to his large muscular snout, just his presence was no doubt enough to make her tremble. She laughed uneasily as Eral pulled her into his embrace to quiet her discomfort.

I thought it might be the octopus as well. He kissed her forehead, before addressing Lacos once more. *Well, my big green friend, what are you doing here?*

With a whip of his tail the dragon moved closer. A frown tipped the corners of his mouth. *Rumor has it that you are now the King of Atlantis.* He shook his big head, his eyes filled with sorrow as his voice softened. *Condolences on your loss and that of your people.* Another slash of his tail drew Lacos even closer. With his sharp werefin senses Eral caught the fishy scent of Lacos' last meal. *May we speak?* His dark round eyes darted left and right as if he felt the coral walls of the cave had ears.

Memories of his own childhood took Eral by surprise. Perhaps coming to this cave was responsible or maybe Lacos' condolences—either way he smiled at the thoughts. Derel and he had discovered this cave of sponges once when they were hiding from Lawl. As boys they were always playing hide and seek, always running away from Lawl when he was in charge. Even then his elder brother had a sense of responsibility, a duty he had never shunned. Eral felt unworthy standing in his brother's shadow.

When Kalina raised her worried gaze to his, Eral pulled his thoughts back to the present. *Yes, my friend, it is safe to speak.*

Lacos' voice dropped to a mental whisper as another stream of bubbles escaped through his large mouth and nose. *An eloin told Camshor—* The dragon hesitated then locked his big, dark eyes on Kalina as he explained. *Camshor is a malamute-crab. Blue eyes, can you believe that? Yes, it is so. Not always responsible. Well, sometimes. Sometimes, yes. But I feel that due to the circumstances—*

Lacos. Eral's grumble held impatience that slid across his skin like the tingle of a jellyfish. The dragon was a friend, but if he did not get on with his story Eral was seriously thinking of spearing the animal with an arrow. Lacos was a gossip and could be frustrating at times, but he was reliable.

The sea dragon stiffened his backbone. The rolls of spines along his back shifted, making him appear even larger. *Yes. Of course. Uh, where was I? Hmmm…Yes! Anyway, Camshor told Harrien, the seahorse,* he glanced at Kalina and then back to Eral before continuing, *that the King of Malachad is behind the death of your brother and the people of Incasha.* Lacos released his breath sending a stream of bubbles upward, then grinned as if pleased with himself.

Eral's fists clenched. Fury, hot and wild, rushed through his veins. *Balin,* he growled, as tension crawled up his neck. *I'll have his head on the end of one of my arrows.*

But there is more. Yes, there is. The dragon interrupted the turmoil churning inside Eral who struggled to fight it.

The brush of a soft hand across Eral's cheek brought his gaze to Kalina. He read sorrow in her eyes. He cupped her hand and brought it to his chest. Just her touch seemed to calm the demon inside him. How did she do it?

More? Eral asked though he did not want to. Instead he wished things were as they had been before.

Yes. The Malachad ruler seeks you. An angelfish swam by, catching Lacos' attention. His forked tongue whipped out, sliding along his jagged teeth. *I have not yet had dessert today. No, I have not.* He shook his head. *Er…where was I? Oh, yes. A human. That is correct. A human.* The dragon paused as the angelfish drew closer. Lacos' nose wrinkled, his eyes closed as he inhaled. *Ahhh…*

Eral's muscles at his neck and shoulders knotted even more. He released Kalina and his large tail made several swipes in the water that carried him so that he was face-to-face with Lacos. *What do you mean when you speak of a human? What are Balin's plans*? He reached out and grasped his friend by the snout and shook. *Lacos, focus.*

The dragon's eyes opened as his stomach growled. *Sorry, my friend. Balin has engaged a sorceress. She took a human and changed him into the monster that killed your brother.*

Kalina looked from the dragon to Eral, her brows narrowed. *A sorceress? Impossible. I know all who practice in this realm.*

Lacos waggled his head side to side. *Well, miss know-all, you are incorrect. That you are. One of the king's* bakirs *has the gift.* The dragon's forked-tongue flicked out catching the yellow, white and black fish as it ventured too close on its final pass. Lacos' eyes shut. He smacked his lips, chewed, then swallowed as an expression of ecstasy slid across his face.

When his eyes opened again, his expression changed to one of concern. *King Eral, the octopus I speak of was last seen close to Atlantis. A poison, it is, the sorceress has created within the octopus that is killing your people and many of the ocean life. I fear if Balin is not stopped the entire sea will cease to live.*

King Eral. Still he could not find it in himself to accept the title so easily.

Eral closed down his mind-link. *Lawl, what am I to do?*

It started with just a spark that Eral felt beneath his skin, and then it increased like lightning ripping through him. He had heard Lawl speak of the King's magic more than once when he had first taken their father's place, but Eral's disinterest had caused his brother to stop the discussion.

Magic.

Ancestral magic. Magic that passed from one ruler to the next upon the death of the prior ruler.

That knowledge and magic surged through his body. He felt Lawl's presence. His father and all the grandfathers and great-grandfathers before him filled him with strength. Their power grew and his body began to glow like a star in the heavens. Light burst from his fingertips as he held his hand before him in wonder.

Kalina and Lacos both gasped at the same time.

Eral could do no more than drink in the energy that made him dizzy, yet caused him to feel powerful all at once. In his heightened state he could have sworn he heard Lawl's voice. *Do not worry, my brother.*

Sand rose from the ocean floor. It swirled in front of Eral, creating one pattern and then another until the outline of Lawl's face appeared. The granules shifted with each movement of the sand sculpture's mouth, along with the cocky lift of one brow—an action that was uniquely Lawl's. *You were always meant to rule. Have faith,* the sculpture mouthed.

Just as quickly as the sand had risen it dispersed and drifted back to the ocean floor.

Then all was quiet.

Eral's mind became a maze, paths leading in all directions. At that moment he knew exactly what needed to be done. Ignoring the disbelief on the dragon's scaly face, Eral said, *Spread the word that the yellow tube sponge soaks up the foul water and replaces it with clean oxygen that is readily available to those within its touch. Invite all to join us here if need be.*

Eral floated to where Kalina stood while he continued to speak to Lacos. *Tell all that the King of Atlantis will rid our home of this threat.*

The sea dragon bowed his great head. He whipped his tail through the water, his small wings fluttering madly. He pushed through the water, disappearing over a towering reef of coral.

Pride sparked in Kalina's eyes. She reached for him and he went into her arms. *It is as it should be. You will succeed,* she said.

Eral did not know if the words she spoke were true, but he did know that where he was at this moment, in her arms, was where he should be. He had no doubt Kalina was his mate, and after the octopus and Balin were destroyed he would make her his own.

But for now there was work to do.

Derel, he called to his brother as he took Kalina by the hand and led her through the seaweed curtain so they were in the cavern of sponges.

Immediately, his sibling appeared. With the aid of the healer and the yellow tube sponges, Derel had made a full recovery. He bowed, his gaze cast downward. For a second, Eral wanted to shake him, remind him that they were brothers.

Equals.

But that was no longer true.

I am *the King of Atlantis*, he thought to himself, letting it flow through him in a powerful wave. He squared his shoulders.

As if his acceptance was heard throughout the kingdom, he felt his people's support envelop him. With a swish of his great tailfin, he turned and stared at the hundreds of werefins before him. Their expressions were grim, but hope flickered in their eyes. He knew he could not ask for anything more after what they had been through. His previous escapades had not warranted their trust and support, but he knew it was there now by the mere fact he had brought them to safety and that he was their king.

It started as a mind-whisper, *Hail, King Eral*. Then it grew into a rumble as they uttered the words aloud. The rumble shook the cave walls and made the water ripple and caused a knot to tighten in his belly. "Hail, King Eral," they said aloud, the words floating through the water.

It was near to overwhelming. For a moment all Eral could do was stare at those individuals with whom he had grown up. Some had taught him many life lessons, while others he had played and caroused with as a boy and young man. When he opened his mind-link to speak they grew silent.

Bubbles pushed from his mouth as Eral spoke. "We all mourn the passing of our King." Eral paused as his frail mother swam to float beside Derel. Eral bowed to acknowledge her. Navara forced a smile that did not reach her red, swollen eyes. Her silvery hair rose in the water and then settled on her shoulders as Derel slipped a protective arm around her. Eral cleared his throat, pushing back the emotion that threatened to surface as he continued, "Even without King Lawl we must remember we are stronger together than apart."

Looking at what was left of his immediate family, his brother and mother, and the people of Atlantis, Eral wondered why it had taken him so long to understand this fact. Godsdamn, he had been a stubborn werefin. He glanced at Kalina and saw approval in her eyes.

"Together, we can rid the ocean of this danger and return to our home. While I am gone you will obey Derel as you would me."

Derel's arm slipped from their mother's waist. Disagreement reigned in the tight lines that furrowed his brow as he stepped forward and mind-whispered, *Nay, it is I who should go and seek the destruction of the octopus.*

Eral ignored Derel's plea. He turned from his people and mind-spoke directly to Derel. *Stay close to the sponges, Derel. Watch over Mother and our people.* He placed his hand on his brother's shoulder. *Should I not return know that I have faith in your ability to rule and that the magic of our ancestors will assist you.*

Speak not of this, Derel protested. *Send me in your place. Let me hunt and kill the monster.*

Eral felt his brother's need to avenge Lawl's death, because he too held that vow deep in his heart. But there was more at stake here. Eral knew it was his fate to confront the demon, as well as Balin.

He embraced Derel, proud of the man his sibling had become. *It is not to be. It is my destiny.*

As it is mine to attend the king, Kalina's mind-spoken words prickled his skin like thousands of needles.

He would not have her in danger.

Eral released Derel and spun to face Kalina. *You will remain here, safe, with Derel and my people*. His tone was short and sharp, leaving no room for argument.

He was king. She must obey.

Kalina's chin rose. She appeared calm, although a vein along her throat pulsed. She called the sapphire from the vault and held the glowing gem in her palms. Within its depths he saw a battle with the King of Malachad. He glimpsed Kalina's face in the stone, but her part in the battle was not clear to him.

Her eyes rose to meet his in defiance. *The stone has spoken. I am to accompany you.*

No. Eral wanted to grab and shake her at the same time he wanted to pull her to him and kiss her senseless even as the stone grew cold and dark.

Fire sparked between them as their eyes met and locked.

You cannot change what is to be, Kalina insisted, a look of supreme confidence on her face.

He reached for her, dragging her hard against his chest, the stone between them. *I will change it. You will remain behind and wait for me.*

No. She inhaled and exhaled and he felt ripples of water skim his face. *You will not leave me.*

Their lips were a breath away when Derel cleared his throat, reminding Eral that they had an audience. He scanned the crowd, receiving curious stares, as well as a knowing smile from his mother. It was the first true smile he had seen on her face since she had been told of Lawl's death.

Godsdamn. He could not take Kalina into danger. He would not. *We will talk about this later*, he mind-spoke to Kalina before addressing the crowd aloud. "I need eight warriors."

Without hesitation, five soldiers that he knew well swam from the throng. Dalpon was a large and boisterous werefin who wreaked havoc wherever he battled. Krueger, Dalpon's twin brother, carried the same reputation. Mawny, a lithe fighter, was as quick with a sword as with a crossbow. The arsenal he carried was varied. Pier, known for his magical lasso in restraining foe, was indeed a pleasure to see. The last was Johas, a young man who was just coming into his own. Eral had heard talk that he was indeed a strength to reckon with. Trailing them were three of Eral's closest friends, Karny, Simo and Taurus. On the outside the men were every inch the carousers Eral had always been, but he knew he could not have three finer warriors. Their tails swished side to side as they lined up in front of him. Each werefin was the vision of what the elite Atlantis Marina stood for—freedom and justice.

Eral hardened his expression. "Make ready. Spend a few moments with your families. Ensure that you carry plenty of the sponges on your person. We leave within the hour."

Kalina raised the sapphire and it vanished from her palm, surely back to the vault. Eral skimmed his hand down Kalina's bare arm and captured her hand. *Now let us settle the matter.* The firmness in his mind-voice made her eyes widen. Good. She was finally listening to him.

Before he took her to a secluded area so they could talk in private, he stopped before his mother. Navara stood regal as a Mother Queen should. She cradled his face in her warm palms.

"Return to me, my son." She never allowed the despair he knew she felt to creep into her voice. Still she trembled when her arms embraced him.

Eral dropped Kalina's hand and returned his mother's hug. "I will, Mother."

Navara released him. He studied her reddened eyes that surely would have been misty if they were not in the water. Navara had chosen to be Mother Queen upon her husband's death, rather than ruling, allowing Lawl to become King of Atlantis.

Navara turned to address Kalina. Their eyes met. Silence lingered as a moment of female understanding passed between them. With a slight dip of her head, Kalina nodded and his mother smiled again. Eral would have given anything to know the meaning, but he probably never would.

Be safe, Navara said before she swam away.

Again, Eral gathered Kalina's hand in his. His body was tense. His thoughts ran in all directions. The witch could certainly be stubborn. He wanted to strangle the woman, but first he had to make sure she remained behind.

Eral had yet to turn back to human form as they pushed through the water, past his people who were settling into their temporary home the best they could. It appeared that a nursery had already been established. The single female werefins were in charge, while the children's parents staked out beds of sponges for their families. Rather than laughter and cries of delight, even the children appeared to know the dire situation they faced.

The muscles in his neck tightened again as he realized the children felt unsafe. Kalina squeezed his hand. Did she feel the same regret?

As werefins adorned with sponges swam out through the curtain of seaweed, Kalina asked in mind-speak, *Where are they going?*

To hunt for food. Eral looked at Kalina and a rush of warmth spread throughout his chest. When had this woman stolen his heart? Curse his father for being right—that one day he would find his mate and uphold his family legacy.

This woman was indeed his mate and he would have her safe, he silently vowed before he continued speaking. *Others are gathering a collection of sponges for us to carry on our journey.* Everyone worked together as it should be. Eral could not be prouder.

Worry creased Kalina's brows. *Going beyond the sponges is not safe.*

Neither is starving, Eral said.

Weaving through cave after cave lit by the magic of his people, he guided Kalina deeper into the maze, until finally they were alone. With just a thought he transformed into human shape, sending his pelt to the vault as he pressed his body to hers.

He breathed in her scent then captured her mouth. At first it was a gentle kiss as he moved his lips lightly across hers. She was so soft, so pliable. His tongue slid between her lips and she opened, inviting him in to taste her. The moment he did, the kiss became ardent, a joining of tongues. He could not wait one more minute to possess her.

Driving her backward, he pressed her against a cushiony wall of sponges, forcing his hips and legs between hers, his cock hard against her belly. He placed his palms against the sponges on either side of her head and prayed for control.

Godsdamn, woman, you are beautiful.

Her amber eyes clouded, her lids heavy with desire. A light, seductive expression slid across her face. Long ebony tresses hid the treasures of her full breasts. He had to see them, touch them and taste them before he left on his mission. With a glide of his hand, he brushed her hair aside. The firm globes fit perfectly in his palms as he cupped them. His thumbs skimmed across her rosy nipples already hard with need. Then he dipped his head, took one into his hot, wet mouth and began to suckle.

Her head lolled back. She sighed, leaning into his touch, a sigh that made a shiver race down his spine.

He pinched, pulled and twisted the taut buds, forcing a whimper from between her parted lips. She was so sexy as she writhed, lifting a leg to curl it around his and draw him closer. Her moist heat slid across him, enticing and teasing him with a promise of pure heaven.

Fuck me, Eral. It was a plea that made him growl and call upon his magic. Instantly he drew her arms away from his neck and pinned them against the wall above her head. She struggled against his hold, but magic flowed within him enforcing his strength. *No! I need to touch you.*

Not now, my little witch. Truth was that he was starving to feel her hands on his skin. So much emotion flowed through her that he could actually sense her desire. Gods, if he only had more time.

She gasped, releasing air bubbles as he entered her in one swift thrust. Immediately, he felt the rush of water between them as he pumped in and out, tilting her hips for better penetration as he plunged deeper. His desperation to brand her, make her his, came through in the heated rhythm he made love to her.

The soft walls of her sex convulsed around him, squeezing him tight. He groaned and held his breath, willing himself to make the moment last.

Eral, please. Please let me touch you. The passion in her voice nearly shattered his control.

Come for me, Kalina. I cannot wait. He raised his chin, opened his mouth and released the song of his people.

Kalina joined with a sweet cry of ecstasy that mingled perfectly with his. As her hips moved, wringing out each sensation of her orgasm, every muscle in his body tensed as he filled her with his seed. Yet he felt her holding back...*something*. Not her ecstasy, but something else, something that rocked the back of his mind.

The errant thought vanished as more of his orgasm ripped through him—gods, he had never experienced anything like what he shared with this woman.

When at last he was spent, he began to relax, until he witnessed the array of colors beneath Kalina's skin. The one in particular that had bothered him before was now an even darker shadow rippling beneath her skin.

Black.

Death.

Either hers or death by her hands.

The ache in his gut was almost too much to bear.

Immediately, he pushed away from her, keeping her arms restrained above her head with his magic. He would not lose her, would not allow her to die. Nor would he allow her to feel the guilt of taking someone's life.

Reinforcing that magical hold on her wrists, he drew away from her. He took one more look at his beautiful woman then kissed her lightly.

My magic will hold you until long after I have gone and then you will be released. Kalina's jaw dropped and he caressed her cheek as he added, *Take care, my love.*

Chapter Eight

❧

Release me! Kalina fought against the magical bonds that held her tight to the wall of sponges as she watched Eral transform into a werefin. *You have no right to bind me, and it is my duty, my* responsibility *to serve the king.*

I will not have you hurt in any way, Kalina. Eral gave her one last lingering look before he swam away.

You have no right!

He disappeared, leaving her hidden where none of the other werefins would find her for now.

Kalina had not felt anger since she was a cub, before she learned to push it back and hide it along with most of her other emotions. She had always kept them under control, had always remained calm and attended to her destiny as sorceress to kings, as it should be.

But now heat flushed from her head to her toes. Her body vibrated and she ground her teeth, fighting for the control she had maintained since that time when she had realized what her future held.

The heated flush in her cheeks only increased. She fought against the magical bonds that held her tight against the wall. *That son of a sea lion.*

The more she struggled, the more she had to fight the natural urge to transform into a weretiger. It would surely mean her death by drowning deep below this godsforsaken sea. She had no idea if the bracelet would remain as her arm shifted to a foreleg should she transform.

And then it happened.

It broke loose.

She felt it start at her toes, working its way up to her calves, her thighs and to her sex. Her breasts tingled and her nipples hardened before it flushed up her neck to her face to the very ends of her hair.

Her long-dormant magic burst from her, lighting up the cave. The surrounding water glowed from the amber sparks flying from her fingertips.

Gods! She had finally lost control.

And…she loved it.

She reveled in it.

It was like a drug that made her want more. Made her embrace the power she had long suppressed.

Sparks flying from her fingertips brightened the water so much that the flash nearly blinded her.

It took nothing to break the bonds. With the sudden jerk and release, Kalina stumbled. She barely caught herself before falling forward. At the same time triumph surged through her veins.

She was finally embracing her heritage. Finally embracing the part of her that she had hidden so well.

Kalina had not known her parents, having been taken from them as a cub before they died. The witch who stole her away did so to exploit Kalina's growing powers. But Kalina had suppressed them, refused to use her magic. No matter how much the old woman beat her, Kalina would not give in. Finally, when she was eighteen, the witch took her from the realm she had grown up in and sold her into underground slavery in Tarok. Almost immediately the king had discovered the underground ring of slavery and freed her. Slavery was not tolerated in all of Tarok.

She had willingly served the four kings ever since—until the last king was mated—and she had promised herself to never use the powers that took her from her family. The Tarok kings knew nothing of her past and respected her wishes to not discuss the matter. She had always been somewhat of a mystery to them, which had pleased her.

But now…this release of her powers…the magic flowing through her felt so right.

It is time.

Kalina started to follow the direction that Eral had led her, but found herself flailing without him to guide her. He had taught her how to kick her legs, but had held her hand while they had navigated the water. How was she going to reach the surface at this rate, without assistance? She doubted that even her newly released powers could help her swim.

Kalina worked her way through the network of caves, stepping on the sea sponges as she went. She passed male and female werefins who were busy at work, doing what was necessary to prepare their new—hopefully temporary—home. She slipped past the werefins, pleased that no one stopped and questioned her. It was difficult navigating, but she finally managed to reach the curtain of seaweed that blocked the view of the open sea from the cavern of sponges.

With both hands she parted the veil, only to see a line of Eral's warriors guarding the sponge refuge.

Return to safety, milady, the closest sentry spoke through their mental pathway. *None are allowed to leave. King's orders.*

Her heart rate picked up and her backbone stiffened. *Eral is not my king. He has no right to rule me.*

The large sentry frowned with obvious disapproval. *When in Atlantis, you must comply with King Eral's commands.*

Heat flushed Kalina's cheeks and she tried to tamp down the anger that was now coming too quickly. She started to respond when she heard a mental singsong humming coming closer. Her gaze shot up to see Lacos floating overhead with what appeared to be a pleased expression—if sea dragons could have expressions.

Eral's guards had immediately raised their bows, but the sentry beside Kalina ordered them to stand down. *It is merely Lacos, King Eral's friend*, the sentry said in mind-speak.

Lacos blinked his great eyes, circled back and slowly came to rest on the sea floor in front of Kalina and the Atlantis guard. His rough green hide glimmered in the water and he was covered in the yellow life-saving sponges. A string of them circled his neck and others were positioned haphazardly over his great body. Kalina would have laughed at the beast if the situation were not so dire.

Lacos winked at her and twitched his pointed ears as he wagged his brows. If she did not know better she would say the dragon was flirting with her. Then his smile faltered as he looked from her to the line of guards.

Where is the king? Lacos asked in mind-speak, his huge eyes wide with concern.

He has left on business. The closed-lipped sentry offered no more explanation.

Lacos blinked, but Kalina spoke before the guard could silence her. *He has gone to confront the octopus in Atlantis then the King of Malachad.*

The dragon shuddered then stilled. *Uh!* The sharp sound of disbelief was followed by the swish of his large tail. *How did I not know of this sooner?* His wings flapped with frustration. *I know everything that goes on beneath the sea. Yes I do. Must be slipping. Need to make the rounds more frequently.*

He left moments ago. Kalina moved away from the guards toward Lacos. The sentry she had been speaking to started to follow her but paused when she stopped to caress the dragon's hide. She leaned against him and whispered her next words in her mind, closing it off to the sentries, so that only Lacos could hear. *I need to be on the shore of the Kingdom of Malachad before Eral arrives. It is my destiny. But I cannot swim.*

The dragon released a breath and bubbles rose up from his nostrils. His gaze traveled up her legs, making her feel strangely inadequate. He cocked a brow. *Yes, I can see why. I can indeed. A tail you need instead of those two things.*

Lacos! Kalina's legendary patience was wearing thin and her shoulders ached from it and from looking up at the giant sea creature. *I need you to take me to the surface. But we must travel fast, faster than King Eral's guard who are watching me now. Can you do that?*

Lacos tossed his great head. *If the king has seen fit to leave you behind, he would not like my interference. No he would not...* His gaze darted to the sentry.

If I do not reach Malachad before Eral does, he will *die. While he deals with the octopus, I must face Balin. It is written in the stone.* Kalina summoned the sapphire from the vault and held it before his great eyes. *My visions never lie.*

More bubbles escaped the dragon's nostrils as he studied the stone. Image after image filtered across its surface. After a moment Lacos gave a nod and sighed.

He squeezed his eyes tight, and to Kalina's surprise, a lump, not unlike the pommel of a horse's saddle, rose beneath Lacos' skin, close to where a group of yellow sponges rested. *You best hurry. The guard is quick, but I am faster. Yes I am.* He grinned, obviously pleased with the fact.

She sent the sapphire back to the vault with a thought. Before she knew what was happening, Lacos' tail swept her up with enough power that she was able to grab the lump at his neck and swing her leg over.

Stop! The large sentry started forward, thrusting his tailfin in the water and speeding toward Kalina and Lacos.

Lacos shot forward so fast that Kalina almost lost her grip on the dragon's pommel. She hung on and pressed herself low, almost burying her nose in the sea sponges that ringed his neck.

For such a huge beast, and despite his tiny wings, Lacos was incredibly fast. He zipped through the water at such a high rate of speed that everything around Kalina blurred. He navigated so quickly that her heart raced with concern that they might run into a great reef or some other obstacle.

Water rushed over her skin and her hair flew behind her. Kalina's cheeks stung from the cold water like a windburn. Her anger dissolved, the tenseness in her shoulders relaxed as they neared her destination. She again pushed her emotions behind her façade of control and calm.

Finally, above her she saw light filtering through the sea. The sun!

We are almost there, the dragon's voice sounded urgent in her mind. *Be prepared for the shift from water to air.*

She barely had time to process that reality as they broke the surface of the water. Kalina tried to breathe, but her lungs and nose were full of water. She managed to hang on to Lacos as she started to puke water from her belly and water came out her ears, nose and mouth as her lungs expelled the salty sea water. She collapsed against Lacos' back as she choked out the last mouthful. She felt pain behind her ears and knew that the gills had disappeared.

For a moment she was so exhausted from releasing the water from her system that she could only lay there, her eyes closed. She truly felt like she'd vomited out all her insides.

"Are you all right, milady?" Lacos' concerned rumble met her ears, and she realized he was talking aloud rather than through a mind-link.

"That was a disgusting, unpleasant experience, but I'll survive." Still holding on to the dragon's pommel, she pushed herself to a sitting position and shook off the weakness that had gripped her from throwing up. The sun seemed so bright she blinked, squeezed her eyes shut, then blinked again. "Just give me a moment."

When Kalina became used to the light, she noticed the warmth of the sun on her back and shoulders. A breeze pebbled her nipples and caused goose bumps to prickle her skin. She rose up to see Lacos floating serenely on the water, a good hundred feet from the shore. He was munching on seaweed as he waited for her to recover. Above the surface of the water he looked more an iridescent blue than shimmering green.

She inhaled sweet, sweet air. There was still some water left in her system that she coughed up after every breath, but she did not care. In moments she would be back on land, where she should rightfully be.

Kalina leaned forward and rubbed behind Lacos' small ears and he gave a deep dragon rumble. A satisfied sigh eased from his mouth as he was obviously pleased at how she stroked him. Kalina straightened and brought both hands to the pommel. "Can you go back to Atlantis to help the king face the octopus? As fast as you can fly through the water, can you reach the city before he does to help protect him? Then bring him here when the octopus is defeated."

"There is much I can do that the king is not aware of." The dragon gave what sounded like a proud snort. "He and his entourage cannot travel as swiftly as I."

Kalina smiled and patted his rough hide. "Will you take me to the shore?"

Lacos nodded his great head, splashing water over Kalina. "Yes I will. I can fly in the air as well as in the water."

While Lacos headed toward the shore, Kalina realized she no longer feared the sea. After everything she had been through since leaving land, it was no wonder. But she certainly would be glad to feel dry soil beneath her feet or paws.

With another deep breath of air, she took stock of her surroundings. Her heart started pounding in her throat as she realized where she was. She had been too busy puking up water to take a good hard look.

A sheer cliff rose up to her left, black rock as hard as ore. Before her was the shore — not the white sand of the beach near Lord Kir's realm, but dirt and rocks, and dark, dark sand. Not a soul was in sight.

Kalina shivered. Lacos had indeed brought her to the Kingdom of Malachad.

When Lacos reached the shore, she patted his neck, careful to not dislodge any of the sea sponges. "Thank you, Lacos. You have done me a great service — and an even greater service to King Eral."

The dragon sighed as she slid off his side to touch the shore in the knee-deep water. He turned his great head toward her and blinked his large eyes. "I trust you, Sorceress Kalina, or I would not have brought you here."

She rubbed his muzzle and he continued, "Keep safe, milady. Yes, you must. And protect King Eral. He is my dearest of friends."

Kalina placed a kiss on Lacos' forehead. His skin was rough but not unpleasant beneath her lips. "I promise." She smiled at the sea dragon before turning her back on him and working her way to the shore. The sand was rocky and the rough stones bit into her feet. Not sharp enough to cut open her skin, but they hurt her feet nonetheless.

When she reached the shore, she turned back to see Lacos watching her. He had moved farther away from shore and he now floated so that she could only see his great back and the top part of his head above the water. Kalina smiled before she began to shift into a weretiger.

Incredible pleasure filled her as the process started. Her body tingled all over and hair rose on her skin from her head to her toes. Her nose and mouth elongated, her eyes slanted and her ears extended. Her limbs lengthened and fur soon covered her now powerful body. She dropped to all fours and gave a low, satisfied growl as the cold breeze off the water ruffled her fur. With a quick look at her foreleg, she saw that the gold band was still on her. She was not sure if it irritated her, or pleased her.

She glanced at the dragon and roared her thanks. Lacos gave one last wave of his tail but still watched her.

Kalina turned away, wanting nothing more than a few minutes to run, to stretch her legs, savor the incredible sensations of freedom. Goddess, she had been below the surface of the sea for so long. So very long. She had yearned for this moment where she could run free and relish being a tiger.

After checking the shore from one end to the other to ensure she was still alone, Kalina bolted down the shoreline. Her muscles bunched with each stride, her legs stretched, wind blew against her nose and face and stroked her fur. She breathed in deep gulps of air, drying away the remnants of the water that had been in her system. Gods, she had never appreciated being a tiger so much until this very moment. Complete abandonment and joy made her blood sing and her body to feel lithe, sleek and invincible.

Yes, she would face Balin and bring him down before he knew what hit him. It was her destiny.

Kalina had never allowed her emotions to run so free. The fact that she had gone from anger to such incredible joy was something she had never experienced before.

The feeling was so heady, so fulfilling—

She was jerked to a hard, painful stop, slamming against an unseen barrier.

A net snagged her, causing her to tumble on the shore.

Rope wrapped around her body, burning against her skin.

The abrupt stop made her head spin as she flipped over. Her heart raced as she staggered to her feet and tried to whirl back the way she had come. But she was entirely surrounded by and tangled in a net of rope.

Kalina snarled, hissed, clawed at the ropes that had taken away her freedom. She rolled within the net on the shore and rock, fighting to get it off her. She bit at one of the ropes, sinking her sharp teeth into it and tried to tear it apart.

As soon as she bit the rope a shock bolted through her and she quickly spit the threads from her mouth.

The rope had to be strengthened by magic. Powerful magic.

She stopped struggling and pushed herself to all fours—

And saw Balin standing beside a red-robed woman on the shore.

Not just any woman. *A sorceress.* She could feel the magic rolling off her.

It was true. Everything Lacos had said was true. There was a sorceress Kalina had not been aware of.

Kalina's seer's senses told her instantly that the sorceress was from the same realm Kalina had been taken from. The Realm of the Trees. A distant place that would have taken months for the sorceress to travel before she reached Malachad.

Kalina growled as she ripped her gaze from the sorceress to Balin. As she had seen in the sapphire stone, he was a handsome bastard with long dark hair, dark eyes and an infinity symbol tattooed on each cheek. It was no wonder Mikaela had fallen under his charm before he ensnared her with his sorcery.

Her breathing came harsh and heavy as she looked at the two who stood on the beach, watching her. Behind Balin and the sorceress was a line of black-robed *bakirs*.

She growled again at the feel of the ropes binding her. The sight of the beautiful woman's smile and Balin's satisfied smirk only intensified her fury.

Trying to control her emotions again, Kalina fought to relax, to tamp down the anger. In any situation, anger was counterproductive. She merely needed to maintain control of her emotions and she would be able to find her way out of this trap.

"Ah, Kalina, the *mighty* sorceress is now mine," Balin said with a hint of laughter in his voice.

The red-robed woman scowled. "Kill her now. We have no use for her."

Balin's gaze snapped to the brown-haired woman. "It is not for you to question me, Letta. Your place is on your knees, sucking my cock."

Letta's scowl deepened. "It was I who predicted this moment would come and that we would capture the bitch. It was I who designed this net. It was I who changed the human John Steele into the great creature we sent to destroy King Lawl and Incasha."

"Remember who your ruler is." Balin took a handful of Letta's brown hair and jerked her head back so that her face tilted up to look at him. An expression of pain passed over the sorceress's features, followed by a sultry expression that Kalina recognized all too well—but to see any woman enjoy submitting to Balin's brutality turned her stomach.

Balin lowered his head and gave Letta a brutal kiss that surely bruised the woman's lips. He then bit her lower lip so hard he drew blood and Letta cried out. When he raised his head he released his hold on her hair and she straightened. The sorceress licked the blood from her lip and gave Kalina a smile full of pure evil.

Kalina found the smile cold, chilling. The woman's eyes sparkled, and the aura of her dark magic deepened, and deepened again.

With a start, Kalina realized just how powerful this sorceress had become—far more powerful than even Balin realized. No wonder Kalina had not known the woman was in this part of the world. No doubt she could use her powers to block any sense of her presence.

More dread trickled through Kalina.

This sorceress, this woman who called herself Letta, was indulging the King of Malachad, allowing him to believe he was in control.

"As I told you, Sorceress Kalina will lure King Eral to us." He wrapped his hand in Letta's hair again, almost absently, and tugged her closer to him. His hold tightened and she flinched. His voice lowered, anger vibrating through every word. "And then I will kill the bastard."

This cannot be right. Kalina tried to tamp down the panic welling within her like a dozen tiny angelfish rising up her throat. *I am to help Eral, not lead him into a trap!*

Balin released his hold on Letta's hair, allowing her to straighten once more. "Now it is time to take our prize to the castle."

Instinctively, Kalina tried to back up, but she was too firmly bound by the net.

Letta's robe flapped open to expose one of her slender, pale legs as she walked toward Kalina, who could not suppress a growl from rising up within her throat. Even if she transformed back into a human at this moment, Kalina's magic would be no match for this sorceress, not when she was bound in a net of thick, magical ropes.

When Letta stood before her, Kalina's vision turned hazy and she unleashed her anger. She swiped a paw through a gap in the net. She extended her claws and in a flash ripped through the flesh on one of Letta's pale ankles.

The red-robed sorceress screamed. Blood poured down her ankle to her foot as she stumbled back. With a look of black hatred, Letta reached into her robe, withdrew a pouch and flung the contents at Kalina.

Kalina closed her eyes and held her breath as the red dust hit her full in the face. But it did no good. Her skin quickly absorbed the powder.

She staggered, opened her eyes and released her breath only to catch the strong smell of poppies and something far more sinister. Her vision blurred as she saw the furious but satisfied smirk on Letta's face. Kalina's hearing became muffled, but she heard Balin's shout, saw him backhand Letta, causing her to fall to the rock and sand.

"Too much!" Kalina thought she heard Balin shout before everything faded away.

Chapter Nine

๛

When Balin backhanded Letta, it was so fast and hard she dropped to the sand. She held her hand to the red mark he'd left on her face and terror flashed across her features.

Fists clenched, Balin tossed back his head and roared. The warriors standing in his vicinity stumbled back in obvious fear. His entire body trembled with fury and he could barely keep himself from ripping out Letta's throat.

Kalina, in weretiger form, lay sprawled on the dirt and rocks beneath Letta's net of magic. Letta's poppy dust covered the unconscious sorceress's white-and-black-striped coat. The weretiger's breathing was so shallow he could not see her chest move.

But he sensed she was alive. Barely.

If she died he would indeed strangle Letta while digging his talons into her slender white throat, bleeding her slowly.

He knew rage blazed in his eyes. All the things he had planned to do to Kalina would have to wait, and he had already waited too long.

His shaking became almost uncontrollable.

Letta's impertinence was inconceivable. Or did she react out of jealousy? The woman knew that his hatred against Kalina was due to the fact that she had helped his wife escape his control. Through her sorceress's abilities, Letta no doubt sensed that he still loved Mikaela, yet Letta had shown her desire to serve in his wife's place. The sorceress couldn't possibly think she would become his queen.

He had thought Mikaela would eventually come to her senses and realize her place was by his side. But instead of returning, she had fled.

No one had ever escaped him until Mikaela.

He gritted his teeth at the realization he was incorrect—that the human, Steele, had indeed slipped his grasp, too, but only temporarily. The weak bastard would not flee a second time. After the octopus-man released his final bladder of poisonous ink, Letta told him the beast would turn back to a helpless human. Steele would drown in the dark depths of the ocean.

This reminder gave Balin some comfort, but not much.

Each time he thought of the Tarok kings—his wife who was their sister—Lord Kir and now King Eral, Balin's blood boiled. The entire kingdoms of Tarok, Oz and Atlantis should be under his control. It was his destiny. His crystal ball had foretold it—

Although it had proven to be faulty in the past. He shook off the doubt that briefly filled his mind.

Balin growled. He spread his arms wide and breathed in the energy crackling in the air from his anger. This was all his and his alone. Wind whipped at his white robe, releasing the sash and splaying the robe wide to bare his nakedness beneath. His erection was firm between his thighs. As his arms lowered he pinned his glare on Letta.

"You disobeyed me." A menacing smile twitched the corners of his mouth. "Your insolence has robbed me of my pleasure." He cupped his cock with a hand. "Therefore, you will receive the bitch's punishment until she awakens. Remove your robe."

Fear raced across Letta's face, enhancing the excitement Balin felt rolling through him. She bared her body, the red robe slipping off her broad shoulders to settle at her feet.

But what was much more satisfying was the woman's terror laced with what he knew would finally be her surrender. She would give him her body with no struggle.

"Do you accept this penance?" He licked his lips, barely able to control the need to dominate the woman before him.

The muscles in Letta's throat worked as she swallowed, hard. Her answer was a simple nod as she began to rise from the ground. Bits of sand, dirt and rock covered one hip and leg, now reddened from her fall. Her cheek still sported his handprint, and he was pleased to see the scratches on her breasts where he had marked her during their earlier coupling. Her bottom lip was swollen from his bite. Blood clotted at her ankle where the weretiger's claws had connected. The coppery scent was an aphrodisiac to his senses.

"Did I order you to rise?" Balin's voice boomed although he savored the thought of one punishment after another heaped upon this woman.

With a swipe of his hand, magic seared the air and pushed her hands from beneath her. As she fell once again onto the rough beach, a rush of air squeezed from her lungs and forced a cry from her lips.

When Letta jerked her head back, she pushed her brunette hair out of her face and he saw fire in her eyes. Her canines elongated as if she readied to shift to her tiger form. Then she paused and the light extinguished from her gaze, her teeth quietly receded.

Her sudden control was eerie and sent a sliver of concern through him. For a moment he wondered just how powerful her ancestry truly was. There had been rumors... Yet if she possessed her ancestors' true magic it would not have taken her so long to discover her powers.

Or had she known along? The fleeting thought had touched his mind before, but he doubted she could have refrained from using it as long as she had.

Still he knew there was no one more powerful than he.

He would use Letta, drain her of her power and then dispose of her. Mikaela would not accept another powerful woman within his kingdom. His wife would return sooner rather than later now that he had Kalina under his control.

Thinking of Mikaela was the wrong thing to do. He had truly loved her. Just the thought of his bride sent heat through his chest, heat of both longing...and hatred.

As his palm began to itch, a six-foot leather whip appeared in it. It felt good to wrap his fingers around the smooth handle. With a snap of his wrist, the tail coiled and then extended, biting the air in front of him. He had expected Letta to react, but she remained calm, lying on the ground before him. She was just far enough away that the sting of the frayed end would make a delightful mark on her beautiful body.

His breathing elevated as he switched his attention to his *bakirs*. "Take the tiger to the castle. Post two guards on her and contact me as soon as she wakes." Godsdamn. How he wished it was Kalina feeling the cutting edge of his whip. Still, he would relish teaching Letta her place.

The unconscious sorceress made no sound or movement as two warriors raised the net and carried her limp but large and powerful form between them. The net was firmly in place, even though Balin knew the drug Letta had given her was enough to cage her power for hours. The *bakirs* carrying Kalina had no fear of the red powder that lost its potency as soon as it made connect with the weretiger. Without being told, his *bakirs* surrounded Kalina and the warriors carrying her. Balin could smell their anxiety at ensuring this woman did not escape them. They knew that he had accepted their failure for the last time.

An air current whipped beneath his silky, white robe, raising it again, as Balin pivoted and drew his attention back to Letta. "Crawl like the bitch cat you are." He thought he heard her hiss as she rose to her hands and knees. Her rounded ass faced him as she began to follow the entourage back to the castle. As she seductively swayed, he realized she was taunting him, begging to feel the lash of his whip. There was something heady about a masochistic woman. In each of their couplings, Letta enjoyed everything he dished out and he knew there were no limits. She had an incredible pain threshold.

With a snap of his wrist the thongs at the end of the whip cut into Letta's hip. Four small tears in her skin opened and blood began to slowly ooze. Her back arched as she released a cry that made Balin's cock harden more. His balls drew up. Blood and seed created a delicious ache between his thighs.

Another flick of his wrist and the whip cut down her shoulder blade making a red path clear down to the small of her back. That one had her collapsing upon her chest to the stony beach. She trembled. Her breaths were ragged as she forced herself back upon her hands and knees.

When she rose, elbows locking, her thighs parted wider giving him a view of the soft, pink flesh of her mons. Balin raised his nose to the air, inhaling her heated desire. She released a purr as her backbone rolled one vertebrae after another. She wanted to be fucked.

As his army disappeared around a corner of trees, he threw the whip into the air and it disappeared with his magic. Letta had begun to crawl again, moving slower than before. With one swift move, he grasped her arm and pulled her to her feet, forcing her back against a large boulder that was snug against a tree.

Letta's nostrils flared. Her silky brunette hair was wild and tossed around her shoulders. "Fuck me, Balin. Fuck me hard and fast."

He twirled her so that her belly pressed against the stone's rough surface. The rock was high enough that he could bend her over it as he pushed her forward, knowing the cool stone would bite into her tender skin. Swiping his hand through the air once more a length of silk rope appeared in his palm. He moved around the boulder and wrapped the end of the rope around her wrists and drew them together. Then he took the other end, circled it around a lone tree and pulled it tight until she was perched on her tiptoes. Then once again he moved to stand behind her.

He ran his fingernails across the open wound at her hip and she hissed. "You have been very bad, Letta."

Her breasts were pressed flat against the stone. "Yes, milord."

He cupped her ass and squeezed. "I will have to hurt you to teach you a lesson in obedience." His cock jerked so that the crown touched her briefly between the thighs and she tensed, as if waiting for him to thrust into her. Just the thought of entering her made him suck in a breath and hold it.

"It is as it should be, milord. My only wish is to pleasure you." Letta's words were correct, but her voice was tight and short. Perhaps it was the discomfort she felt pressed against the ragged rock.

Without any preparation he thrust cruelly into the taut entrance of her ass, tearing through the rings of muscle as he pushed deeper inside her. Gods, she was tight, so very tight.

The scream that ripped from her throat threw him immediately over the edge. His leaden weight pushed her hard against the rough surface as he collapsed against her back. Every muscle clenched in his body as his seed exploded like a flash of fire that burned down his cock. It was painful and thrilling all at once. His heart pounded mercilessly. His pulse raced. She trembled and whimpered softly beneath him. But not once did she complain or beg him to stop. For a moment he simply lay there buried deep inside her body.

As he felt himself soften, he slipped from her warmth and used his magic to cleanse himself. He should have felt sated, but he was not. He stepped back and looked at the woman draped across the boulder. The tendons in her shapely legs were stretched. Her skin was covered with a light film of perspiration and blood still ran from the cuts he had inflicted upon her with his whip.

No matter her pain, he knew a sweet ache existed in her reddened rosebud and she was wet and ready for him to fuck her. But she deserved every punishment he wished to dispense and he had no intention of satisfying her needs in any way. She had robbed him of beating and fucking Kalina. For that she would pay and pay dearly.

He took one last look at her bound form, drew his robe closed and fastened the sash around his waist. Then he began to walk toward the castle leaving Letta to think about the distress she had caused him.

"Sire. You do not mean to leave me here?" Her voice rose sharply.

He ignored her and continued to make his way to his castle.

"Balin!" she screamed. But for some unknown reason he felt tired. Even when she yelled, "Bastard," he felt unmoved to discipline her further.

Balin was weary of failure. It seemed those around him were incompetent and unable to follow a plan through to its end.

"But not this time," he vowed aloud.

King Lawl was dead.

Incasha was destroyed.

Steele was heading to Atlantis to annihilate Eral and all his subjects.

He smiled.

And let him not forget what the crystal ball had told him—no matter with Letta's assistance.

The orb had revealed that the sorceress Kalina was headed straight for his trap.

Chapter Ten

ഇ

The water seemed colder than normal to Eral as his tailfin moved up and down, slicing through the ocean's currents as it carried him forward toward Atlantis. His skin prickled, a sharp electric sensation, as the tiny hairs on his arms came alive. Was the cold just his imagination or was it guilt for leaving Kalina bound and alone in the cave of yellow sponges? She was so deep inside the cavern no one would hear her cries for help. She would not be bound too long—just long enough for him to be too far from her for her to find a way to catch up.

Or perhaps the water seemed chilly due to the fact that Kalina was not by his side. Visions of her warm body pressed against his made him long to be in her arms. Instead he and his men each carried a bag of yellow sponges around their waists, along with swords, crossbows, quivers and a variety of other weapons strapped to their chests or hips.

As he passed a pair of gray stingrays, he recalled the shock on Kalina's face when she realized what he had done. He had deceived her with a moment of pleasure. His actions lay like a heavy weight in his chest. It was for her own good. The woman was headstrong and unable to see the wisdom in his choice to leave her safely behind.

Truth was he had had to hold her before he journeyed off to the unknown.

Thoughts of her anger as she struggled helplessly against his magic bindings swamped him. He nearly collided with a mountain of sand peaking up from the ocean's floor at the straying of his thoughts. He knew her anger now would be nothing like the fury he would face when they met again. He swerved, even as his tailfin sent a cloud of sand into the water.

A pissed-off sorceress was not something he looked forward to.

He and his warriors had only been gone for about an hour. Another hour would put enough distance between them that Kalina would no doubt come to understand the dangers of trying to follow. Even if she managed to free herself, he knew she could not follow since she could not swim.

First he would rid the ocean of the threat the octopus posed, and then he would settle the score with the King of Malachad.

Just the thought of the sorcerer who had once imprisoned Eral's mother a few years ago made his anger boil. Her health had never been the same since her captivity. Now the death of Lawl and many other werefins lay at the bastard's feet.

Eral felt the rush of water as Karny moved beside him.

Atlantis is our destination? Karny asked using the mind-link of their people. His thick brown hair looked like a chocolate veil floating behind him beneath the water. His eyes were an even darker shade than his hair. He was one of the favorites among the female werefins and many of the female werewolves, too.

From the corner of his eye, Eral caught a flash of Taurus' blond hair as he swam to Eral's other side.

Of course, Taurus said to Karny with a scowl. *We hunt the octopus. No need to swim aimlessly in search of the beast. His destination is Atlantis, so shall it be ours.* Taurus shook his head. Eral's blue-eyed friend was built like a Tarok bull and hung to match. He was the brunt of many well-endowed jokes, but the truth was that he was envied by many a werefin male.

Only one woman was on Eral's mind, and if she would not have been endangered, he would have had her by his side.

Godsdamn, he cursed silently and looked behind him even though he knew she would not be there. Instead he saw the two younger werefins guarding their backs. Eral only hoped that when his bonds eventually let Kalina go, his sentry could detain her. If she found some way to leave the safety of the werefin encampment, then he would have more than a word or two to say to her when next they met. She had much to learn about obedience before becoming his queen.

You appear anxious, my King.

Taurus' formality caused Eral to grit his teeth. This was a man with whom he had shared many a fine lass. Together they had had their fill of drink and had stayed out for long hours. Now he spoke to Eral as if…as if he were king.

Eral forced back a sigh of frustration. He *was* king.

Anxious? Of course not. I face the annihilation of our entire race every day, Eral snapped then immediately felt chagrined by his surliness.

Forgive me, Eral said through mind-link with his friend. *I have yet to come to grips with the loss of my brother and so many of our kind.* Not to mention attempting to bear this new role as king, he thought to himself. *I simply wish for you to treat me as you always have*, he added to Taurus.

Karny gave Eral a wicked smile. *You mean to match tailfins and fists to see who can take who down to the ocean floor?*

Taurus frowned, tossing Karny an uneasy expression, before he said, *It cannot be, Sire. You are our king. We serve you.*

Well, at least Karny had not changed. If Eral needed to be knocked down a peg or two he could count on at least one friend to do it with pleasure.

And what about this Tarok sorceress we have seen you with on numerous occasions? Karny asked, elbowing Eral in the side. *Will you be sharing?*

Touch her and I will beat you into the ocean floor. Eral's answer came too swiftly and with too much emotion behind it.

Karny and Taurus shared a bewildered expression, and then Karny burst into laughter. *Our friend has been caught in his own net of desire. His days of freedom are at an end.*

Amusing. Eral smirked and then grew serious. *Kalina is my soul mate. We will be bonded once Balin is safely out of our lives.*

A weretiger? Disbelief rang in Taurus' mind-voice. *I mean…congratulations, Sire.*

Kitty, uh? From the grin on Karny's face, Eral knew he had some off-color comment perched on his tongue.

Do not say it, my friend, warned Taurus. Then he and Eral began to laugh. They both knew Karny only too well.

Time passed while they worked their way toward their former home. And hopefully it would be home once again.

As they neared Atlantis they grew quieter. Four warriors went ahead of Eral while two guarded their backs as they swam through the caverns to reach the city.

Atlantis was like a graveyard, void of any movement or sound. There were no laughing werefins — no life existed among the place he had called home.

Eral's head ached with both fury and sadness. He had the uncontrollable urge to slam his fist into anything — anyone.

Then he heard it.

A burble came from behind a large wall of orange coral just to the north of Atlantis' entrance. The sound was coming from the base of the coral, near the sand.

The shadow of something large peeked from behind the coral and began to rise.

Heart thumping, Eral raised his crossbow. His men moved in tandem with him.

Eral tamped down the anger that burned in his chest. But the magic of his ancestors rose within him. It sizzled up and down his arms and spread across his entire body. Confidence filled him, not only his own, but that of his brother, his father and all his grandfathers before him.

He cocked his bow and aimed his deadly arrow toward the mass of coral, waiting for the moment of revenge. The minute the octopus showed its ugly head, nine arrows would pierce its heart—if it had one.

He knew his men would wait until his command, and that command was soon in coming.

A form darted from around the coral.

Eral's arms tensed as he readied to unleash his arrow—

A trigger fish.

Another rustling sound behind the coral. Louder this time.

As one, Eral and his men snapped their aim back toward the coral as a huge mass exploded from behind it.

Eral's heart stopped.

His body thrummed as he prepared to loose the arrow. He held a second.

Eral's men held for his command.

His fingers locked.

When the form burst from the shadows, relief rushed through Eral in a burst of air from his lungs, causing bubbles to float in front of his face. He lowered his crossbow.

Godsdamn, that sea dragon.

Lacos caught sight of them and abruptly stopped, making skid marks in the sand.

Golgee! The animal's scratchy voice crackled. His eyes were as big as giant sand dollars. Air bubbles blew rapidly from the dragon's flaring nostrils as he scanned one arrow and then the next aimed at his chest. His breathing was erratic by the rattles that squeezed from his chest. His wings were aflutter, only a blur within the water.

We almost killed you, Eral growled in mind-speak. Acid rolled in his stomach. Even though he was certain his men should never do so without his command, what if one of his warriors *had* released his arrow?

Lacos appeared to be paralyzed. He did not move or speak other than that one word. His rough scaly hide was a putrid green instead of his usual vibrant mossy shade. If he had not been so angry, Eral would have been amused at the sight of all the yellow sponges dotting the dragon's hide, and the ring of sponges around his big neck.

Staring death in the face could knock a man off his feet. No doubt even a sea dragon could feel that way, which could have been why Lacos looked so stunned. But there was something more in Lacos' tortured expression that chilled Eral straight to his bones.

The other eight warriors lowered their aim from Lacos. The men shifted their stances and stood ready, each searching with their gazes for their prey. But Eral could hear their comments of dismay over the big dragon's abrupt appearance.

The bag of yellow sponges pulled against his waist as Eral swam toward the dragon. *Apologies, my friend. We are simply on edge due to the task ahead of us.*

When Lacos was finally able to speak, he said, *I just witnessed it, yes I did. The octopus is no longer a threat to the ocean. No he is not. But…*

Eral hated the "but" word. He tried to have patience with Lacos. The dragon meant well. However, the creature's hesitation was more than Eral could stand. *But,* what? he asked.

It was amazing. Amazing it was. Lacos paused as his eyes rolled. *Yes it was. His belly looked burned, as if by some kind of magic. I watched as a cloud of black trailed behind him. He sought the beach. He did.*

Eral felt a sense of relief brush the weight from his shoulders. *He is dead?*

Dead? Oh far from it, my King. An eel slithering through the water caught Lacos' attention. The dragon slid his tongue over his pointy teeth.

Did Lacos think of anything but his stomach? Eral pushed his tailfin through the water and swam up to come face-to-face with the sea dragon. He thumped the creature on the nose with his crossbow. *Focus, Lacos.*

Ouch! The action made the dragon bite down on his tongue. He flicked his injured tongue out several times and took a moment to gather his thoughts. *Yes. Yes, indeed. No, not dead. Changed.*

The sound of that last word sent a wave of unease through Eral.

Lacos' gaze followed the eel for a moment longer and then drifted back to Eral. *He is human once again. But unlike any human I have seen.*

When the dragon paused again, Eral raised a brow in frustration, urging the sea dragon to continue.

Strong. Muscles. Four arms. I witnessed him lifting a boulder, large one at that, and toss it out of his way. Yes he did. Lacos whipped his tail in the sand. *The magic and poison must have seeped into his system. Yes, that would be my guess.* Again the dragon hesitated. *Uh…Eral… The human did not look happy. He was heading in the direction of Lord Kir's realm, Emerald City.*

Eral clenched his teeth. *Steele is the only human that I know to exist in Tarok, except for the kings' wives. He must know that Awai, his ex-wife, still remains in Lord Kir's realm while her husband, the King of Clubs hunts him,* Eral said.

I will track him down, Eral added with determination. It mattered not where he killed the beast who took his brother's life, just that in the end he was dead. Then he would deal with Balin.

No time. No time, indeed. The dragon eased away from Eral. Lacos' eyes shifted from side to side. His posture tensed as if he would bolt at any moment. *Before I witnessed the octopus change to a man… The sorceress, the one you call Kalina, she was taken.*

The dragon's words were a knife slicing through Eral. *What? How? She is at the cave of yellow sponges.*

Not exactly. Lacos cringed. *I took her to the surface. I am far, far faster than werefins, I am. She sought to fight Balin. I saw it in the stone.* Lacos spoke quickly and then said, *But…*

Every muscle and tendon in Eral's body clenched. He tried to prepare himself for what he knew was coming.

She was overtaken by the King of Malachad moments after she arrived on shore, Lacos finished whipping his tail side to side, putting further distance between them. *I watched from the sea. I did not know what to do but find you. But before I came here, when the sorcerer had left my sight, and then his sorceress, Letta, that is when the octopus-man crawled from the sea, he did.*

Eral felt like a tsunami was erupting inside him, building larger and larger, driving him to the ocean's floor. The ground itself shifted below him. He planted his tailfin and waited for the earthquake he knew would follow, but did not. It was only his emotions and the thoughts of Kalina within Balin's evil grasp that caused his world to tilt.

He drew on his strength and turned to his men. *We go aground.* Eral did not wait as he began to swim furiously in the direction of Balin's kingdom.

I can take you there quicker than you can swim. Yes I can, Lacos chimed, releasing a stream of bubbles from his nostrils.

Eral was willing to hear any suggestion that would get him to Kalina faster. *I am listening, but make it fast, Lacos.* Eral's hesitation allowed his men to catch up with him. They were grumbling about plans and keeping the king safe. Eral refused to listen. His only thought was Kalina.

On Lacos' back two lumps rose near the long stretch of his neck and another one a couple of feet down the dragon's spine. *Two can ride upon my back. The rest can try to hold on to my tail, but it will be a difficult task. Difficult indeed.* He preened as if he knew something they did not. *I shall come back for those who do not make this trip.*

Extraordinary, Taurus said, as he swam to the second pommel and ran his hand across the hump. Taurus loved horses. Eral knew the thought of riding was an exhilarating proposition for Taurus.

Taurus shall ride with me. The rest of you secure yourself to Lacos' tail, Eral commanded.

Sire, should we not devise a plan before striking out into danger? Pier asked.

Eral did not have the luxury to pause and consider a plan. Something inside him knew that Kalina would not see the evening stars if he did not get to her this day. *You may refuse to attend me — that shall be your choice. But I go now, with or without you.* Eral flexed his tailfin and swam to the front pommel, gripping it to sit sideways. Taurus seated himself behind Eral, holding on to the second pommel. He also sat sideways so that his tailfin was positioned on the opposite side of Eral's. *You have but a second to decide and then we leave.*

No one required the second as they attempted to clutch portions of the sea dragon's wide tail while avoiding dislodging the yellow sponges arranged haphazardly.

Ouch! Watch those arrows, Lacos cried. Then he took a breath, whipping his tail side to side as he cut through the water.

It was beyond anything Eral could imagine. Moving through the water at such high speed made his head spin. Atlantis was a blur, a spot in the distance, and then gone. Nothing was identifiable at the pace they traveled. His cheeks sunk in and then flapped with the give and take of pressure squeezing them. He heard a muffled groan and had no doubt that they had lost one or more of his men. If he did not have the pommel to hold on to he, too, would have been left behind.

When light crested the surface of the water, Eral's stomach pitched. Pier was right that they needed a plan — he had been reacting rather than thinking the situation through. Even with his eight warriors there would be no way to get through hundreds of Balin's *bakirs*.

But that would not stop him from trying.

They broke from the water so quickly he did not have an opportunity to empty his lungs underwater to prepare to surface. A breeze caressed Eral's face as he gasped for a breath. The shock made him clasp his hands around his throat. It felt as if he was choking to death. Then that precious moment when his gills closed and air flowed naturally through his system occurred. Quickly he sent his pelt to the vault, legs forming as the dragon slid across the surface.

With a hand, Eral shielded his eyes from the bright sunshine. By the alignment of the sun in the sky, he realized it had to be midday. They continued to break through the waves moving toward the shores of Malachad.

"Godsdamn. That ride set my heart to racing," Taurus crowed, a light of excitement sparked in his eyes when Eral glanced back at him. "Let us do it again."

"Who of the men made the ride?" Eral asked aloud.

The soft voice that spoke surprised Eral. "It is I, Johas." The young warrior was adhered to Lacos as if he was glued to him. Blue sparkles danced around Johas as he released the dragon.

Pier's glowing blue magical lasso was looped around Lacos' tail. Holding on to Pier's feet was Karny.

The annoyed expression on Karny's face said it all, but he obviously had the need to express it. "I do not *ever* want to do that again," he grumbled before morphing from werefin to human. Pier retracted his lasso and began to check his weaponry.

Five of them had survived the trip to land.

"I will retrieve your comrades." Lacos smirked. Eral could not tell whether the look of pride on the sea dragon's face was due to assisting them, or losing the others. "Lost four we did. Expected more. Yes I did." He waited for Taurus and Eral to dismount and then he dove beneath the blue-green depths and disappeared.

They were approximately twelve feet from the unfriendly shores of Balin's kingdom. Eral's arms stroked and his legs kicked furiously, as he closed the distance between him and Kalina.

Where Lord Kir's beach was silvery white sand, the dark sand of Malachad was a mixture of dirt and jagged rocks that would have pricked at his feet if his soles were like humans and not like the tough hide of a werefin.

To his right the rocky beach stretched on, and in the intermittent sand he saw the prints of a tiger that looked as if it had been running. He frowned at the coarse bindings he spotted laying upon a large boulder, as if something had been strapped there. Rust-colored spots dotted the boulder—like blood.

Eral's heart set to pounding even faster. Could that have been Kalina's blood? The vision of black that had been included in Kalina's last orgasm came to mind. No. She could not be dead. He would not believe it. His gaze scanned the beach further where he saw that there had been some kind of struggle in the dark sand that had once been smooth, but now had dips and grooves.

He ground his teeth and tried not to let his emotions overcome him. That must have been where Balin had taken Kalina. But was she the one the sorcerer had strapped to the rock?

Eral was going to kill Balin.

As fury welled inside him, he forced his attention back to his task. A line of trees sprang up in the distance hiding the gray-stone castle to the left. The castle perched near the sheer cliffs that rose high, black and forbidding. The castle he had stalked once before in his lifetime. His memory was like a book as he paged through it, remembering how Lord Kir had slipped through the hidden passageway beyond the gates to enter the castle in order to save Navara, Eral's mother. Surely that passageway had been demolished or now riddled with magic to ward off trespassers.

Then it dawned on Eral. "Pier. Can you use your lasso to get us over the wall undetected?" For the first time since he heard of Kalina's capture he felt a wisp of hope.

"It can be done, my King." Pier bowed, his features pinched. Pier was a strategist. Clearly, this impulsive approach was not sitting well with him.

Eral tapped into his warrior skills as he stealthily began his journey toward the castle. "Then we must search for the least likely guarded area."

Using his magic, Eral called forth from the vault soft leather boots, breeches and a vest, and left the bag of sponges on the ground. They would not need them now. He called across the mind-link with the other four men and suggested they do the same. The terrain of Malachad was not pleasant. Not only was the ground uneven and the rocks sharp, but the trees and bushes seemed to reach out and tear at the skin.

The trip was as difficult as Eral had expected before they entered the treeline. Balin's magic in the air was not easy to fend off—the evil closed around them like a jacket one size too small. It thickened in their lungs causing Eral to feel nearly suffocated. It left an odd, bitter taste upon his tongue. Eral pulled from within him the image of a shield that folded around him and his men. With the magical shield created from the newly acquired ancestral powers he now wielded, he and the other werefins would be safe from the foul air, as well as the tentacles of power Balin extended over his land.

Eral knew his presence would be expected, but if the gods were on his side the swiftness of Lacos could have bought them a little time.

Still their pace was slow, too slow. The closer he drew to Kalina the more Eral's skin prickled. *Halt.* He used his people's silent method of speech as six black-robed *bakirs* on patrol, riding horseback, crested the hill that lead up to the castle. Eral's fingers itched as they rested on his crossbow. He saw the same unease and readiness on his warriors' faces.

When Eral and his men reached the outskirts of the castle wall, Eral held his hand up, again halting his men. "Pier and Johas, go left. Survey the perimeter for a weak spot. One that will allow us to crawl over the wall undetected." They nodded and without comment held their crossbows at the ready and departed.

Eral watched them for a moment then he, Taurus and Karny veered to the right. On featherlight steps they avoided the keen eyes of one *bakir* who stood atop the battlement while scanning the terrain. His gaze landed in the direction of Eral and his friends. The three froze.

Time ticked slowly. The beat of Eral's heart was loud, thrumming in his ears as he waited to see if they had been detected. When the *bakir* turned and walked the other way, Eral released the breath he held.

Once again he scanned the imposing gray walls of the castle. Eral attempted to push thoughts of Kalina from his mind. He had to focus, had to find some way inside. But she was always in his thoughts. What he would give to have her in his arms.

The light snap of a twig caused him to spin around. Pier and Johas had returned.

Karny gave a hissing sound. "Godsdamn, Pier. Could you and Johas be any louder?"

"The walls have to be twelve feet high," Eral said, ignoring the exchange between the two men. "The battlement has guards posted on all sides."

"It is the same on the other side," Pier added.

Eral released a frustrated breath. "There has to be an unattended space we can crawl over." But there was not and he knew it.

As a unit, they began to backtrack.

A soft whistle caressed Eral's ears. It was Dalpon's signature call. Through mind-link, Eral let the werefins know where he and his men were now located.

When the other werefins joined Eral's group, Karny grumbled, "It is about time." Restlessness rippled across his face. The werefin was not a warrior to wait for trouble. He sought it. Eral was impressed with his friend's control.

"Perhaps a little inside cooperation would be of value." Mawny reached inside his vest pocket. When he opened his hand a miniature Lacos appeared on his palm. The sea dragon waved his wing in greeting. Even the yellow sponges that dotted his body and hung around his neck had shrunk to a miniature size. All Eral could do was stare. "It would seem that your friend has many abilities." Mawny raised his hand and Lacos took to the air, buzzing like a bee around Eral's head.

"I have come to help. Yes I have." Lacos landed lightly on Eral's shoulder. Eral's eyes crossed as he looked down at the tiny sea dragon. He never knew Lacos contained such magic. "How can I serve you, King Eral?" Lacos' usually loud, scratchy voice was tinny and high-pitched.

Eral did not know how much a dragon this size could do, but surely he could get past the *bakirs* unnoticed. "My friend, thank you. Can you find Kalina? Tell us where she is being held?"

"That I can do." Lacos' wings became a blur as he rose high above Eral's head. Then in a flash he zipped one way and then the next, before he darted for the castle—but not before teasing one of the *bakirs*. Buzzing around the man's head, the dragon avoided the hands of the *bakir* as he brushed his palms several times before his face, swatting at Lacos as if he was a pesky insect.

Anger flashed across Eral's features as he bellowed, *Enough,* using his mind-link with Lacos. In a trice the dragon made his way through a tower window.

The silence squeezed Eral's chest like a vise. With each minute that passed he felt the turn of the clamp, tighter and tighter, until he thought he would scream. As his men held sentry, Eral's thoughts of what Balin's intentions were for Kalina were a constant gnawing in his gut.

He had to get inside. He had to save Kalina.

It seemed like hours before Lacos returned, but it had only been perhaps fifteen minutes at most when the sea dragon buzzed into view and landed on Eral's shoulder.

"The sorceress does not wish for you to risk your life in saving hers," Lacos said in that tiny voice. "It is a trap for both you and the Tarok kings' sister."

Eral pushed off from the rock where he had been sitting. The speed at which he stood tossed Lacos into the air. Anger exploded inside Eral. The heat of it swarmed up his neck and face, touching his ears. How could Kalina think that he would simply leave her in Balin's captivity? The evil bastard would keep her alive only until her usefulness ended, and then she would no doubt die a horrible death.

"No," Eral growled. He would not leave Kalina to face Balin alone. Not to mention the fact he was certain he could not live without her. Just this short time they had been apart tore at his heart. He needed her beside him.

Lacos' wings fluttered madly as he hovered before Eral's face. "You are to listen, my friend. The sorceress is wise. Yes she is." Eral swatted at Lacos and barely missed as the sea dragon darted away. "Tsk. Tsk," he clucked and scolded. "She said you would not listen. Stubborn, she said you were." Lacos barely missed another brush of Eral's hand. "So her next instructions were to retrieve the sapphire from the vault. It is her hope that it will assist you in your time of need. Do it. Do it *now*, for you are in need."

Eral did not like the tone of the dragon's last words. The stone was not his to command, but perhaps he had gained some power over it when he had touched it to share a vision with his beautiful witch.

As Kalina had recommended, Eral held out his hand and envisioned the stone in the pelt vault.

At first, nothing happened.

He pulled back his hands and pushed them before him once again, palms skyward.

His fingers tingled, numbness starting at the tips. But the sensation died as quickly as it appeared.

Again he forced his hands forward. Again, the tingle surfaced and nothing more.

"No," he uttered in desperation. He would not fail her. He would not lose another person he loved.

Closing his eyes, he focused and reached within himself, holding on to his thoughts of Kalina, the stone, the magic.

Once again he called forth the stone. He opened his eyes. The area above his palm flickered, and then shimmered as the gem took form. Immediately, it turned hot. As he brought it before his face, different shades of colors swirled in its midst before clearing and revealing an image. He could see Kalina in weretiger form stretched out in a cage. Her eyes were closed.

She had to be all right, because Lacos had just spoken to her. Right?

Then Eral saw why she faked unconsciousness. Balin was in the room. He paced before the cage. Stopped.

Then he reached to open the door of the cage.

Eral could not help his growl as the stone grew cold, misty, and then the vision disappeared. Nor could he stop the pounding of his heart in his throat, knowing the danger his little witch was in.

The sapphire grew gray, then the gray vanished like smoke vaporizing in the air. Images in the stone began to appear again. This time the stone showed him pictures of the castle, the grounds, a village, people, horses, the *bakirs*, along with the guards along the battlements. Images that could help them in gaining entrance to the castle.

Then he saw Balin again, reaching for Kalina, reaching…

Like a flame taking its first breath, emotion rose fast and furious in him. It was hot and angry, lost and desperate. It churned, growing larger and larger, forcing his mind into a thick haze that blinded him to rational thought. The only thing he could think of was Kalina. He had to save Kalina.

Eral took a deep breath and his vision cleared, but his muscles remained tense and his body burned with his anger.

No. He could not react in a manner that would endanger his men as well as Kalina. He was king. He had to think like a king. He had to act like a king. Proceed with a well-organized plan.

Eral took another breath, attempting to draw courage from deep within. "With the knowledge the stone has given us, I believe I know of a way to get into the castle. Lacos can assist us."

His men stood proud and strong, prepared to do as he commanded. Prepared to give their lives to complete their task.

Each moment that passed was precious. Thoughts of Balin's hands on Kalina were like claws slicing through Eral's chest as he discussed his plan with the men.

It had to work. It *must* work.

Chapter Eleven

❧

Thankful the sorcerer had not come into the room when the tiny Lacos had visited her, and that her two guards had not noticed him, Kalina relaxed somewhat. Lacos would deliver her message to Eral. Surely he would listen?

Yet within her heart, she knew he would not. He would endanger himself to save her and to destroy Balin.

Kalina forced herself to remain in tiger form and fake unconsciousness. Her eyes were closed as she heard the soft footsteps of the two guards as they departed. Now she sensed Balin's nearness, caught his foul odor mixed with wolfsbane and nettles. If he opened the door to the cage, she would be on him so fast his last dying memory would be of her ripping his throat out with her claws or her massive jaws.

The viciousness of her thoughts shocked her. Such deep feelings had been released with her magic and she knew she would never contain the magic or the feelings again.

"Open your eyes, bitch." Balin's voice was low and cold. "I know you are awake. You cannot fool this sorcerer."

Narrowing her gaze, Kalina opened her eyes to mere slits and let out a low growl. Balin rose to his full height, his white robe hanging straight to the floor, obscuring his feet. His arms crossed his chest and a smirk lifted one side of his mouth. He was an incredibly handsome man with dark hair to his shoulders, dark eyes and the infinity symbol tattooed on each cheek that she had noticed earlier.

Kalina could see why Mikaela had been seduced by Balin, why she had become the Queen of Malachad—before he had used his mind-control and forced her to almost kill her brothers and their mates. Before she had escaped and now ran free of his mental grasp.

As she let out another low growl, Balin laughed. "That is right, bitch. You are mine to do with as I please."

Kalina slowly pushed herself to her feet, but staggered. The sleeping powder the sorceress had used against her still lingered in her system. Her vision blurred and she struggled to focus while she analyzed her surroundings. She was in a circular room, obviously a tower. A single door was open on one part of the wall, and three tall, wide windows were fashioned around the tower, the midday sun spilling through them casting rectangles of light across the floor. Over the low sill, she could see aqua-blue sky and even the beach from the window Lacos had flown through earlier.

Her gaze turned to the room and she growled as she recognized instruments of torture and splatters of blood next to them. Chains and clamps hung from one curved portion of a wall and the ceiling, and it smelled of rust and damp rock. Another curve held whips along with floggers with spiked metal balls on the ends. A pair of large iron clamps, obviously meant to pinch—perhaps even tear—nipples, was among other clamps. Countless other items including an assortment of ropes were fastened next to them. In the room were also stretching bars, tables and more.

In Tarok, Oz and no doubt Atlantis, similar but kinder devices would be used to enhance play and pleasure. Here, in this twisted, dark place with this twisted, dark man...*gods*. She did not want to consider.

Suppressing a shudder, Kalina finished getting to her feet. When she was firmly on all four paws and she felt her strength returning, she let out another rumbling growl, louder this time.

The sorcerer only looked at her with increasing amusement as she started pacing. She moved back and forth in the black iron-barred cage, trying to think of some way to overcome the bastard. Seeing Lacos in tiny form earlier had shocked her, but that shock turned quickly to fear when the sea dragon told her Eral was here and planning to make his way into Balin's castle. It was up to her to handle the sorcerer before Eral was hurt...or killed.

"I have waited a long time for revenge upon you, sorceress." Balin reached into the folds of his robe and brought out a handful of a strange-looking powder. Kalina's heightened sense of smell caught a sickly sweet odor like burnt sugar. When he held out his palm she saw brown powder and paused in her pacing. Her heart pounded even more. "You took my beloved bitch from me and have somehow kept her safe from my mind-touch. For this you will pay."

Before Kalina could blink, Balin threw the powder in her face. She let out a feline roar of pain, sat back on her haunches and instinctively pawed at her eyes. The substance went up her nose, choking her, burning her lungs, and she could feel the powder rushing into her bloodstream.

Suddenly she was no longer using her paws to rub at her eyes. They were her hands...her tiger hair was being absorbed back into her skin, her features were shifting, her body becoming human again—

She could not stop the transformation.

Kalina struggled to maintain her tiger form, but before she knew it she was naked and human, the bracelet still on her wrist. Her long black hair flowed over her shoulders to the small of her back and covered her breasts as she sat back, her ass resting on her calves. The burning in her eyes and lungs slowly dissipated, but now she felt almost high instead of lethargic. Her body was jittery and her teeth nearly chattered from the sensation.

"Much better." The amusement in Balin's voice and eyes was gone, replaced by cold, cruel calculation. He raised his hand and slowly passed it in front of him, palm facing the cage. The lock and chain fell away to clatter on the stone floor. "Get out."

Kalina met his gaze head-on. She refused to let the bastard intimidate her. She thought about refusing him and not getting out, but she knew she had a better chance of escape outside the cage.

Not to mention she now wielded a power he could have no knowledge of. He thought of her only as a seer.

Her body shook from the jittery sensation the powder had given her as she crawled on her hands and knees from the cage. When she was out she was staring directly at Balin's toes that peeked from beneath his white robe. Before she had a chance to rise, the sorcerer leaned over. In a swift movement, he placed his hand on her neck, firmly at the base of her head. He shoved her down so that her lips and teeth met the cold stone floor, hard. Pain shot through her mouth and teeth, but she made not a sound.

"Kiss the feet of your executioner, sorceress." Balin yanked her by bunching his fist in her hair and jerking her forward so that her face was against his robe, her lips pressed to the top of his foot.

Kalina shuddered with revulsion at the feel of his cool flesh against her mouth, but with the instinct of her species she dug her teeth into the top of his foot, ripping the flesh. He shrieked with pain as blood met her mouth.

With a roar he flung her away from him so that her naked body slid across the floor. The murderous look in his eyes and the sight of blood staining the hem of his robe gave her some measure of satisfaction—until she realized how helpless she was. She tried to shift, but the powder was still working, preventing her from transforming and disemboweling the bastard.

She tried using her newly reawakened powers that had filled her in the cave Eral had left her in…but nothing would come to her.

Kalina spat on the rock floor and wiped his blood from her mouth with the back of her hand. She had always remained calm, in any situation, but not this time. No, not now. Fury built within her, so strong that her body shook with it.

Too fast for her to react, Balin reached her and jerked her to her feet by her hair. He was so much taller than her that he was able to dangle her by her hair and she felt some of it rip from her scalp. The pain in her head was a flash that blended with the anger building within her. Her toes sought to find purchase, but merely brushed the cool stone of the floor. She was eye to eye with Balin now, and she fought to keep her features calm and the rage from her gaze.

Balin smiled again, and it was even worse than before. As she dangled he reached up with his free hand and twisted her nipple so hard her eyes would have watered if she had not been so thoroughly trained in the art of BDSM. She had enjoyed sexual pain with bondage countless times, but now she was only repulsed.

"Yes," he said in a vicious growl as he twisted harder. "You will soon die, but not before I do to you what I would be doing with my *wife* had you not taken her from me. And not before I *break* you."

She found her voice. "No matter what you do to me, you will never break me, Balin."

She felt more hair tear from her scalp as he raised her higher. His dark eyes were filled with hate. "I will fuck your mouth, your quim, your ass while I whip you until blood flows freely from your body."

Kalina's heart stuttered. He threw her from him so that she stumbled, her ass and lower back slamming against the cage. Rough metal bruised her bare skin and she choked on the breath that stuck in her throat. The ache in her scalp and back was nothing compared to the fury boiling in her veins.

Balin brushed a clump of long strands of her hair from his palm and it floated toward the floor. Her gaze did not follow it. Her eyes remained fixed on the sorcerer's as a rough length of twine appeared in one of his hands, the flogger with the tiny spiked metal balls in his other.

Her body flushed with cold and her veins filled with ice as her mind rushed through her options. She tried shifting again but her body remained jittery and she could not transform. And her magic—useless.

Or was it?

He took a step forward as he raised the flogger.

Before he could flog her, a burst of magic flowed through Kalina. She dropped to her knees and dove beneath the sorcerer's robe so that she was beyond his knees. Catching him off guard gave her the opportunity to swing her fists up. With all her strength and another burst of her formerly dormant magic, she jammed her fists against the backs of his knees.

At the same time she rolled away, Balin shouted his surprise as he toppled backward on his ass.

Kalina scrambled back just as the sorcerer was getting to his feet again.

Fury distorted Balin's once handsome features. With a flick of his wrist he struck her with the tiny spiked balls on the end of the flogger.

Kalina's head reeled from the pain of the blow across her shoulder and back, the flogger making deep wounds in her skin upon impact. She remained crouched as he raised the flogger again.

While his arm was still raised high, she swept out one leg, putting more magic into her movement. Pain shot through her as her ankle connected with his.

The force of her strike knocked Balin's feet out from under him.

A cry blasted from his mouth as he fell backward, arms flailing, flogger and rope dropping from his grasp.

His head struck the stone floor. A sickening crack echoed through the tower room.

The sorcerer's head lolled to the side. He did not move. Only the slow rise and fall of his chest told her he was still alive.

Kalina did not pause. She pushed herself to her feet and grabbed the rough twine the sorcerer had intended to use on her. Blood flowed from her wounds as she straddled him, grabbed his large wrists and bound them with the twine, and used her powers to fully secure it. The magic made the bonds glow a bright white. She knew if not for her magic, he would easily break his bonds when he awakened.

Her magic ran freely through her veins now and she could almost grasp the power to shift.

When she finished binding Balin with the ropes and her magic, she ran for the door.

She came to a dead stop.

The sorceress from the beach blocked her path.

The red robe she had been wearing was now wet and sandy. Through the open front, red talon slashes marked each breast, and her chest, belly and mons looked rubbed raw, as if she had been dragged across a rough surface. At the bottom of one ankle were the claw marks Kalina had left. Her once silken hair was tangled and windblown.

The woman's expression was murderous. She stood in front of one of the enormous windows. A gust of wind came through the window, causing the sorceress' hair to float about her face.

Kalina swallowed as she faced the sorceress and tried to analyze the situation. *Letta. That is her name.*

"I have had it with this pretense." Letta spat out the words as she pointed to Balin's body. "I have far greater powers than this excuse for a sorcerer."

"I know," Kalina said softly. "I knew it from the moment I saw you on the beach. You are from the Realm of the Trees."

A look of shock crossed the woman's beautiful features and her jaw dropped. "How — how?" Her expression hardened again and she raised her chin. "He dies now. You die now."

"We can leave together," Kalina said as she took a step forward and Letta raised her hands. "You can join me and my comrades and become one of us."

The sorceress gave her a look of complete disdain. "I will replace Balin and rule the *bakirs*, along with all that surrounds Malachad."

"There is no way you can do that." Kalina drew on the powers within her. She could not allow Letta or Balin to harm another person. It was time for it all to end.

Letta's fingertips crackled and she gave a smile. It somehow made her look beautiful despite her unkempt appearance and the wild look in her eyes. "Oh, sweet one, but I will. Perhaps I shall even keep you for sport."

Kalina's hair stirred about her shoulders and rose from her scalp as her own power filled her veins even greater than before. She still could not shift, but the powder no longer suppressed the magic that lay within her.

Behind her she heard a low groan and knew that Balin was awakening. She could not fight them both. She had to finish this with Letta, *now*.

Before Kalina had a chance to act, fire crackled from Letta's fingertips and shot across the few feet that separated them. Pain racked Kalina's body as the magic burned into her bare skin. It did not leave a mark, but she felt like she was burning up with fever.

Her survival instincts and her own powers kicked in. Hands clenched at her sides, Kalina sent a mental wave straight at Letta. The sorceress gave a cry and surprise etched her features as she slammed into the wall next to the window.

She recovered so quickly it was as if Kalina had done nothing more than give Letta a light push.

This time a blast of light engulfed Kalina. Her body was on fire! From the roots of her hair to her toes. Pain beyond pain.

Kalina expected to fall to the floor in a pile of ash. But again not a mark appeared on her skin. She felt winded and as if her skin was cracked and peeling, but she stood her ground.

Letta's eyes were wide with disbelief. "You should have died."

Kalina let a slow smile spread across her face. "How did I know you were a powerful sorceress when I first saw you? How did I know you were from the Realm of the Trees?" Her own magic doubled within her core. "It takes one to recognize one."

Despite the obvious shock on her face, Letta raised her hands again, but too late. Kalina's magic slammed into Letta. The sorceress screamed, a high piercing screech that stabbed at Kalina's ears. She stumbled back against the window. The shock on Letta's face turned to terror as she lost her balance and teetered across the ledge.

"No!" Kalina sprinted across the short distance separating them, but Letta was already falling.

Kalina reached the window in time to snatch the sorceress's foot. Kalina clung to the ankle of the screaming and flailing woman who hung above sharp rocks. "Be still!" Kalina cried. "I have you!"

But the sorceress's body jerked hard and she slipped from Kalina's grasp.

"Noooooo!" Kalina threw out a net of magic, trying to stop Letta's fall.

It was too late.

All she could do was watch in horror as the sorceress fell, fell, fell…

Letta's body slammed into the rocks below. She lay still. A broken doll.

Kalina buried her face in her hands as tears flowed from her eyes. "Oh gods, oh gods, oh gods!"

Letta was dead.

Kalina had killed her.

A roar caused Kalina to swing around to face Balin. He was charging her, his hands free of the rope and her magic, murderous rage in his eyes.

She did not have time to use her power to protect herself.

Balin grabbed her by the throat, but the force of his movement sent them both across the window ledge and Kalina over it.

Kalina could not even scream. She was being strangled to death as Balin hung half over the ledge, most of his body still within the tower while she dangled over the rocks. She clawed at his fingers. Her throat was closing off, her mind spinning, his furious features blurring in and out.

"You die now, bitch," he said in a hideous voice.

And dropped her.

She was falling.

Falling.

Falling to her death.

As she had murdered Letta, she was going to die the same way.

Regret for so much flashed through her mind as she fell. Regret for taking a life.

Regret for not being able to tell Eral that she loved him.

She fought for the calm that she had maintained all her life as she prepared to slam into the rocks.

Instead she slammed facedown onto something large and scaly.

Hold on, came a voice in her mind. *Yes, you must. Hold on, hold on.*

Kalina was so shocked she almost slid off Lacos' back. His wing caught her at the same time she flipped over and grabbed his pommel. His scales felt rough to her bare skin, but she welcomed it.

Above she heard Balin's bellow of rage. She cast a glance over her shoulder up to the tower window where she saw the sorcerer. She could not help but put all the fury she felt into her expression.

Lacos continued zipping away, into the cover of the nearby forest as she turned away from the sorcerer.

"Lacos." Kalina could barely speak after nearly being strangled to death. Her voice came out harsh and scratchy. "Thank you. Oh, gods, thank you."

You are welcome, yes you are, Lacos said then paused. *But it is my fault you were captured by the mean sorcerer. That it is.*

"No." Kalina patted the side of his neck that was still ringed by yellow sponges that had now hardened, their soft flexibility gone. "I made my own choices."

Lacos gave a harrumph, but said no more.

All of Kalina's hurts let themselves be known at the same time. The pain in her scalp from Balin dangling her by her hair, the pain of him throwing her at the bars of the cage, the pain of the metal studded flogger, the pain of the blasts of Letta's magic, the pain of almost being strangled to death. But most of all, the pain of causing another being's death.

Yet at the same time she felt relief at being alive. Relief that she would be able to help Eral, Mikaela—everyone who mattered. She would fight beside them to make sure Balin never hurt another soul.

Kalina collapsed with exhaustion against Lacos, her face buried in the sponges. She was barely aware of him flying into a forest and dodging trees. He came to an abrupt stop as he landed, and she lost her grasp on the pommel. She was falling again, but this time she was caught in a strong embrace.

In the next moment she was looking up into Eral's face. He looked furious and relieved all at once. Kalina was too exhausted to say anything. She did not have to speak. Eral held her tight in his embrace as he took her mouth in a harsh, demanding, possessive kiss.

She melted into the sensation, taking everything and wanting more. She felt the roughness of the weapons crossing his body, his human breeches, and the hard press of his cock against her bare belly.

He finally drew away from her, his breathing coming harsh and ragged. He still looked angry. "Do not *ever* scare me like that again. Do not *ever*—"

Kalina cut off his words by putting her hand over his mouth. She managed a tired smile as she said, "I love you, too, Eral."

Obvious shock at her words drove his head up and his jaw dropped.

"I love you," she whispered again just before she collapsed and everything faded away.

Chapter Twelve

ജ

Balin's outstretched hands were paralyzed in front of him as he stared down from the castle window at the large green dragon that swooped beneath the sorceress, breaking her fall. Kalina's long hair was like a veil surrounding her as she flailed for a second before clutching the demon's pommel. With a toss of her head her face was revealed. It softened with relief as her cheek lay flat against the dragon's scaly body. Her relaxed expression lasted only a moment as she raised her gaze and she met Balin's eyes.

Fury was mirrored in her amber glare.

Once again he had been robbed of revenge.

Balin threw back his head, opened his mouth and released a roar loud enough to shake the rafters. It echoed across the courtyard rousing a flock of *eloin* from their nests high in the trees. The colorful birds dotted the cloudless sky in flight over the woodland in the late afternoon sky.

Balin's fingernails elongated into sharp, deadly talons that scraped against the stone windowsill. He grasped the ledge, rage blinding him and his body shaking with fury.

Suddenly, he lunged forward, hands and feet scrabbling recklessly onto the ledge. He drew himself into a tight ball, perched and ready to leap into the air and tear the bitch from the animal's back. But the dragon was quick—its tail whipped side to side like a snake cutting through grass as it darted away from the castle, shot over the treetops then dove into the forest below.

Balin's gaze dropped and a new round of fury caused him to nearly choke as he sucked in his breath.

Letta's broken body was splayed upon the rocks below.

A renewed sense of anger slowed his breathing, helped him to focus as he jerked his gaze to the grove of trees where Kalina disappeared. Carefully, he scooted from the ledge and stood before the window once again.

Another failure.

This one at his own hands.

It was a foul taste upon his tongue. The weight in his chest was even heavier. He had become overconfident in his magic and the brown powder he had prepared. There had been no doubt in his mind that he could trap Kalina's power — that was until he saw her battle Letta. For a moment that power had frightened him as he watched the two sorceresses exert their supernatural forces against one another. Both displayed strength he had not known existed, not only in Kalina, but in Letta as well.

Balin's nostrils flared. What had Letta said as he had tried to regain his senses?

"I have far greater powers than this excuse for a sorcerer."

She had lied and hid her magic from him. Something he had not thought possible.

Godsdamn. What was happening? It felt like his world was splintering. He blinked hard, drawing his attention back to her still form below. Wave after wave of fury rolled over his body. Her betrayal was a knife to his gut.

"Bitch!" he growled, anger warring with a thread of uncertainty that crept along his spine. The moment of doubt only enraged him further.

Another woman had deceived him.

Once again he began to tremble. Fury so hot his body felt like a bonfire, exploded inside him. His own power began to simmer, spark around him in bright fiery flames. It grew in strength, covering him like a coat of iron. The air shimmered around him, and then died.

First Mikaela and now Letta.

He drew his robes and tightly around him and tied the sash. He had planned to use Kalina to draw Mikaela to him. With Letta by his side he had thought he could control Mikaela, convince her that her place was with him.

He had not wanted to face the truth…but the truth was he missed Mikaela.

With heavy strides, he began to pace the stone floor. It was cool beneath his bare feet. The rough edges pressed into the calluses that covered his soles. He remembered the sweet flowery scent of Mikaela's hair, the fire that burned in her eyes and the feel of her soft body beneath his.

His cock hardened with the thought of dominating and being dominated by her. He cupped himself and hardened further as he strode from one end of the room to the other. The cage he had held Kalina in was empty. The scent of blood hung in the air from their struggles. Yet, he was alone with his jumbled thoughts.

Mikaela had been the only woman who had been able to bend him to her desires. He drew to a halt. The tail of her whip had felt so good against his skin. He arched his back remembering the sting, the way she would soothe the burn away with the touch of her lips. The memory made his balls draw up tight. A shiver raced along his backbone as he chased the need for her away. His love had been a weakness, a weakness he had every intention of annihilating once she was in his control again.

"I will have you again, my love." His voice took on a strange eeriness that surprised even him.

The truth was that his wife's magic had strengthened. Or had it been Kalina all this time? He had to admit that Mikaela's magic was electrifying. It was the type of power that made him heady with the need to control. What he could do with both Mikaela and Kalina by his side was unimaginable. The two women would also be beyond satisfying in his bed once he controlled their minds.

He shook his head needing to clear his thoughts of the bloodlust building beneath his skin. These two women had done more to break his will than he wanted to admit.

For months Mikaela had successfully avoided his *bakirs*, as well as the mental fingers of magic he had sent out to discover her whereabouts.

And now with Kalina's escape, his hope of finding Mikaela was shattered.

The realization made him succumb to self-doubt once more. His jaws clenched tight. "Enough," he ground out between his teeth, but the sensation crawling across his skin remained.

It lessened him as a man, as a powerful sorcerer, to admit that he needed Mikaela. He needed her powers combined with his to fulfill his destiny of taking over all the kingdoms surrounding him.

With a sudden movement, he jerked his shoulders back, his spine rigid, his chin raised. Confidence streamed through his veins like a gush of liquid fire.

It was his rightful place to rule.

It was his right to have Mikaela at his side.

Balin was yanked back to reality, when the courtyard below came alive with screams from his *bakirs* and from the peasants in the village.

Horns blew as one of his guards from high upon the rampart announced an incoming threat.

Balin ran to the window, leaned out and looked across the courtyard. Men and women flooded the area. He glanced toward the wall and his gaze followed the path of several *bakirs'* fingers as they pointed to the forest. The trees shook as if the earth was going to split apart. Then the beast that had stolen Balin's revenge burst through the treetops like he had been propelled. Tree limbs and leaves flew into the sky behind him and then dropped like lead. The dragon made a large circle above the grove then moved with harrowing speed toward the castle.

Balin's heart skipped a beat. He flinched. The reflex only made him angrier. Still he held his breath.

The beast's presence seemed larger this time, growing in size as it neared. Bright orange and red flames shot from its nostrils as it whipped its powerful tail side to side, propelling itself through the air.

Balin's fingers curled into fists. "I will not be defeated."

The beast opened its mouth and the most excruciating sound emerged. The high-pitched wail made Balin want to cover his ears. His eardrums pounded from the pressure created by the dragon's cry. They were still ringing as Balin projected his thoughts to his *bakirs*.

Kill the bastard! Shoot to kill! He would have the beast roasting on a spit before morning.

Balin's *bakirs* on the wall readied their bows, aiming their deadly arrows at the menace shooting fire into their midst. The warriors on the ground pulled their swords from their sheaths and took their stances. For a moment the sky darkened as the beast passed beneath the sun, casting a shadow over the castle. Then the creature opened its mouth again. Instead of the ear-shattering cry as before, a thousand needlelike projectiles shot forward.

Several of Balin's *bakirs* screamed in agony as the missiles struck, sizzled and released a blast of smoke. The smell of burning flesh filled the air as the guards fell to the ground. One warrior tumbled over the wall and crashed to the jagged rocks below.

"No!" Balin's now dirty robes swished around his ankles as he spun and moved toward the door. "By the gods above I will kill you—but not before making you suffer the most incredible pain you have ever experienced." His threat echoed through the pathways of the castle. His feet slapped loudly against the stone floor as he reached the stairs and began his descent.

When he rounded the stairs leading to the lower turret, Balin came to a halt.

The King of Atlantis stood at the bottom of the stairs.

A quiet rage hardened the werefin's features as he aimed his crossbow at Balin's chest.

Chapter Thirteen

80

Nothing could have prepared Eral for coming face-to-face with the man responsible for so many deaths.

Midway down the stairs the sorcerer stood motionless as if in shock.

Heart pounding and rage tearing through him, Eral aimed his crossbow and released the deadly arrow. It cut through the air, hissing toward the sorcerer's heart. The rush of satisfaction, of vindication, surged through his veins.

Simultaneously Balin raised his hands.

His clawed fingertip sparked with an eerie purple light.

The arrow Eral had released from his crossbow splintered as it came in contact with Balin's magic.

Godsdamn!

Eral whipped another arrow from his quiver and nocked it. He paused. Unless he caught Balin off guard an arrow would not kill the bastard. It would take more — much more.

Muffled battle cries and screams raged outside in the courtyard, but Eral's attention was focused solely on Balin.

"Your reign of terror has come to an end." Where Eral found the calmness in his tone, he did not know. "You are a disease infecting everything and anyone you touch. You feed on the weak and kill the strong to take that which is not yours. Today it ends."

A wild light filled the sorcerer's eyes and a cruel grin slashed his face.

A door behind Eral slammed open and sounds from outside rushed in. Behind Eral swords clanged. Men and women warriors shouted and screamed. The musty scent of weretiger *bakirs* met Eral's nostrils, but a familiar werefin war cry assured Eral that Taurus guarded his back.

Balin's canines lengthened, the sharp points pressed against his lips as a menacing grin raised the corners of his mouth. His red-rimmed eyes beamed with laughter. "You think that you can defeat me, the King of Malachad?"

Balin formed a ball of purple light between his hands.

Without pause he slung it.

Eral dropped his crossbow.

At the same time, Eral flicked his wrist and flung up a shield of ancestral magic.

The area before him turned glassy and shimmered like rippling water.

When Balin's force struck the buffer, the sorcerer's magic exploded into sparkles of velvety light that rained down upon Eral.

Before he could reinforce his magic, the sorcerer slung another ball of purple fire.

This time Eral felt the sorcerer's power radiate through his shield, hands and arms. It burned across his body and his strength faltered, shaking him to his core.

In a desperate attempt to gain time, Eral opened his mouth and released the magical song of his people, but it was as if Balin could not hear him.

The sorcerer released another projectile.

It exploded against Eral's defense, singeing the remainder of his protection away.

Raw anger rolled across Eral's sweat-dampened skin. A vow rose into his throat. He would not die at the hands of this menace. Taking a deep breath, he drew upon all the energy in his body. A white light appeared before his eyes, blinding him.

The song of Eral's people filled his head. At first it was a murmur, a blend of voices that rose in unison. Then familiarity greeted him. Lawl, their father, grandfather and all his ancestry that came before him sang and chanted, lending him their eternal power and support.

It was a slight tingle beneath his skin, a warmth that seeped into his very bones. Then as if it were a flower bursting open beneath the heat of sunlight, magic surged through him sending lightning shards within. The sensation ricocheted from head to toe, growing stronger and stronger. The power and strength shook him, almost took his breath away.

The sounds of fighting around him dulled. He focused on his enemy and the magic within that called to him.

Eral sucked in a deep breath. As he did he raised his hands into the space above him. With a roar, he pushed werefin magic in Balin's direction.

The force slammed into the sorcerer. It threw him up and backward and flung him onto the landing above. Eral heard air rush from Balin's lungs, the crunch of bone on impact. A cry of pain tore the air.

With a shaking clawed hand, Balin used the wall to scrabble for purchase.

Balin thrust himself into the air and soared toward Eral like a bird.

The sorcerer's mouth was wide open. Razor-sharp teeth twisted the feral look on his face. His fingers curled into claws.

He crashed into Eral. They fell, hard. Locked in each other's embrace they rolled across the stone floor. Eral's quiver of arrows bit into his back. His sword and the dagger at his ankle pressed unmercifully into his skin.

For a moment, Eral's hands were tangled in Balin's robes. Even when Eral freed his hand from the material, he realized that their close proximity allowed neither of them to reach for their magic. Doing so would run the risk of harming themselves as well as the other.

It became a fight of strength—except when Eral felt Balin's tentacles of mind-control.

Like something dark and evil slithering beneath the surface, Balin probed in an attempt to invade Eral's thoughts and concentration.

The dark fingers of power were met with Eral's counter of white energy that made the darkness dissolve.

Eral heard more people swarm into the room, sounds of more swords clanging, but he centered his attention on the man whose neck lay beneath his fingers that pulsed with ancestral magic.

Balin's right fist slammed against Eral's cheekbone. Adrenaline rushed through his veins as he felt his skin tear just beneath his eye. He reacted by releasing his hold on Balin's throat and swung his fist in an uppercut beneath Balin's chin. As the sorcerer's jaws snapped together, his teeth made a sharp grinding sound.

The sorcerer released a roar, slamming his head into Eral's. Stars burst behind Eral's eyes as pain shot toward the back of his skull. He wrapped his arms around Balin, keeping his enemy close as he struggled to chase the bright lights and ache away. Just a fraction of time was all he needed to regain control of his senses.

"Your sorceress was a wild one when I whipped and fucked her," Balin hissed, breathing heavily, his mouth close to Eral's ear. Balin's words and the brush of warmth across Eral's skin sent an even more violent bolt of anger through him. "She screamed for me to fuck her over and over again."

Just the thought of this vile bastard touching Kalina made Eral want to rip the bastard's gut out. Eral pulled his knees up and thrust out, sending Balin from his grasp. The sorcerer landed on his back but pushed himself immediately to his feet. He raised a threatening hand that crackled with purple magic then froze as he looked beyond Eral.

His magic fizzled away.

Balin's eyes widened as he said, "Mikaela."

From the sheath at his leg, Eral slipped his dagger into his palm. Without a second thought he flung it. The blade spun from point to handle through the air, its blade catching the light before it buried deep into Balin's chest.

The sorcerer howled. He stumbled back as he looked down at the hilt. As he grasped the handle and pulled it out, he staggered. The dagger clattered to the floor as a fountain of blood flowed from the open wound. As he fell against the wall, he pressed his hand against a stone.

"Mikaela," he whispered, still clutching his chest with one hand.

Eral's attention was pinned on the sorcerer. He could feel the sweet taste of retribution upon his tongue as he quickly bent to retrieve his crossbow.

Stone scraped against stone. Eral thought of nothing but Balin's death as he nocked an arrow into the bow and aimed it at Balin's chest—this time he would hit the sorcerer's heart.

Before Eral could release his arrow the wall behind Balin swung inward to reveal a passageway.

Balin stumbled into the dark corridor.

Eral loosed the arrow and it vanished in the blackness.

Had it struck Balin?

Had the knife to the sorcerer's chest been enough to cause his death?

The only thing Eral truly knew was that the sorcerer was escaping.

Eral's heart beat faster and blood surged through his veins. He bolted for the entrance.

Balin would not escape.

As Eral's hand touched the cool stone he swore he would see the sorcerer take his last breath. Only then would Lawl, Kalina and many others be avenged.

"Do not follow him." A female's voice slid across his skin like silk as she issued her warning. The calmness in her tone made him glance quickly over his shoulder.

His attention went immediately to Kalina standing next to the woman who spoke. Kalina looked calm and mysterious as always. Her wounds had almost healed, which meant at some point she had shifted into her tiger form. For a brief moment anger flared. Had she been fighting the *bakirs*?

Godsdamn, he missed her. He wanted to go to her. Hold her in his arms. But the darkness behind him was calling. He moved to turn around when the woman spoke again.

"Do not enter." With a subtle jerk of her head she tossed her long blonde mane behind her.

Eral recognized this one all too well. Except for the neckline that exposed the swells of her breast and ran down the front to her belly button, the tight, black leather outfit covered her completely. Her signature was the tattoo of a tiger's paw surrounding her navel. Once one met the Tarok kings' sister, he could never forget her.

"The passageways are riddled with traps." Mikaela's voice was strong, sure. "You cannot fight Balin within his own castle."

The room had gone silent, except for the heavy breathing of the *bakirs* who lay beneath the blades of his men. Karny wore a huge smile as he urged one of the *bakirs* to move and make his day. A dark-haired man stood in the castle's doorway. Lord Kir had introduced the mysterious man to Eral when he first arrived in Emerald City. Rafe was the werewolf's name. From what Eral understood, the werewolf had taken it upon himself to ensure the safety of the Tarok kings' sister and Kalina when they had left the King of Clubs' realm.

For his protection of the two women, especially Kalina, Eral would be eternally grateful.

Eral looked at Kalina and then turned to gaze into the dark space between the parted walls. *No.* His fingers curled into fists. Not this time. He trembled with anger as he took a step. The King of Malachad's life could not be spared. It was the bastard's time to die.

"Heed Mikaela's words." Kalina's voice tightened and he glanced again over his shoulder. "Please, Eral, do not enter." She took a step forward and held out her hand. "If he lives, we will fight him another time. Together." Kalina's eyes went misty. Eral had never seen her cry. Gods, he doubted if anyone had ever seen her cry.

Mikaela joined Kalina. "Old magic is woven throughout. The only way to defeat him now is to bring down the castle. Can werefin magic do that?"

The Queen of Malachad raised a brow. She was taunting him.

Kalina placed a hand on Mikaela's arm, silencing her friend. Then she looked at Eral. "Please, do not go in there." She bit her lower lip and for the first time she looked unsure of herself.

Eral tossed down his bow and opened his arms. Without hesitation Kalina hurried forward into his embrace. Her soft body melted into his. Godsdamn, but he had too many clothes on. He wanted to feel her naked skin pressed to his. He thought of how he almost lost her. She grunted as if he held her a little too tight. She was supposed to be far away from the fighting, not in the middle of it.

"Do not ever do that again." He choked on unexpected emotion that felt like a vise around his throat. She was alive. For the moment Balin's threat was over.

Kalina jerked, attempting to pull out of his arms, but he held her close. "Do not do what? Disobey you?" She stiffened in his arms.

"Well, there is that." He released her so that he could gaze upon her beauty. She gave him a haughty yet angry expression. It was amazing the levels of change he had seen in her within such a short span of time. She had gone from resolute sorceress, confident and serene, to a woman experiencing deep feelings and emotions for the first time. A woman who he would never let forget that in the heat of battle she had proclaimed her love for him—a werefin. He cupped her face with both hands. "But what I speak of is you declaring your love and then fainting before I had a chance to respond."

Her eyes widened. "I did not faint." She squared her shoulders and jerked her chin from Eral's grasp. "A sorceress never faints."

"You fainted," Karny teased from the position he held standing above a *bakir*. He jabbed the man, who was stuck in between human and tiger form, with his sword. "Dead away you did. While you were out we all had our wicked ways with you." He chuckled as Taurus threw him a look of disapproval while Eral glared.

A purr left Mikaela's full lips. "Interesting." She eyed both Kalina and Eral curiously, then turned and flashed Karny a coy grin. The growl from the dark-haired man—Rafe—who was guarding the castle entrance made her frown.

"Psst." A hiss filled the room. "Psst. Are we through here?" A large set of flaring nostrils appeared before the portal. Lacos moved his head so one large eye peered inside. "Ah…it is as I said it would be. Yes it is. Yes, indeed. King Eral is well and whole."

Rafe's movements were a blur as he slid beside Mikaela. Eral did not miss the exasperated expression she tossed the man's way.

Still there was unfinished business here. No matter how much he needed to be alone with Kalina, needed to feel himself buried deep inside her warm, wet body, Balin was somewhere within the walls of the manor.

"Status," Eral asked Lacos.

Lacos shrank so that he ducked his big, green head and entered the castle. "Dead, gone or captured. Yes they are."

"Your friend has a way of clearing a room—or courtyard in this case—with just his presence," Karny said as his roguish gaze smoothed over Mikaela.

Again, Rafe growled. The deep gravelly warning left no doubt that he meant to kill any man brave enough or stupid enough to touch the Queen of Malachad.

"Stuff it, hairball," Mikaela muttered, before she turned and faced Kalina. She cupped Kalina's hand with hers. "My friend, if you are not in need of me I must leave."

Sadness spread across Kalina's face. "Where are we to go?"

Eral's eyes narrowed. If Kalina thought to leave him, she had a surprise coming. He had her within his grasp again. He would not—could not—let her leave.

Mikaela's face softened as she drew Kalina's hand to her face. She closed her eyes and rubbed Kalina's palm gently across her cheek. Then her eyes opened and she placed Kalina's hand in Eral's. "I go alone this time. You have commitments here."

Mikaela leaned close to Eral and growled. "Hurt her and I will eat you while your heart still beats." When she pulled away her blue eyes were moist. She swallowed hard, before taking a step back and coming to a sudden stop when she bounced off Rafe's broad chest. She wiped angrily at a single tear that dared to roll down her cheek. "Wolf boy, I said, 'I go alone'. Now stand aside." She ducked his outstretched hand as he moved to grab her.

Then her body began to contort, snow-white hair emerging from her pores, muscles popping, as she transformed into her tiger form. Sleek and beautiful, the white tiger shook her tail once in Rafe's face before she bounded through the open door and disappeared.

Karny grinned as he clicked his tongue. "Here, kitty, kitty."

If looks could kill, Karny would be dead from the fire blazing in the dark-haired werewolf's eyes. Rafe was quick to change to wolf with a solid black coat. As he leaped toward the door his nails clicked on the stone floor.

From outside there was an immediate exchange of a deep howl, a couple of cat screams and a few barks, then all grew quiet.

Kalina moved against Eral. He took her into his arms and pressed his lips lightly against her forehead.

Taurus cleared his throat. "Your Majesty, not knowing the King of Malachad's condition, we court danger if we remain."

Eral glanced toward the opening in the wall. It was not coincidental that the door remained open. Balin had wanted him to follow. If not for the Tarok kings' sister he would probably not be holding Kalina right now.

Taurus was right about the danger in remaining. Still it went against Eral's grain to leave a job unfinished. Thoughts of Lawl made his eyes sting. He had failed.

Kalina placed her hand on Eral's chest and gazed into his eyes. "His time is near. But it is not now. It is not your destiny to rid the world of Balin at this time. Besides, your friend, Lord Kir, is in need of your assistance. The sapphire told me the human, Steele, is nearing his kingdom."

Godsdamn. Eral had forgotten the threat that lingered, not to his people but to others he held dear. "Lacos." The dragon's wings blurred as he shrunk to the size of a small bird and rose into the air. He hovered before Eral's face. "Can you find Steele?"

Lacos set back on his tail as he nodded. "Yes. Yes, indeed, my King." Then he darted right and left before he flew through an open window.

Eral's hand slipped from around Kalina, sliding down her arm until he held her hand. "Let us make haste." He tugged her toward the door.

"What about the *bakirs* we captured?" Taurus asked.

Eral stopped, turned and looked at the men sprawled across the floor. They had been instruments in Balin's terror. He struggled with his need to avenge Lawl's death. Still he had witnessed the strength of Balin's mind-control. In the past these men and women had served as pawns in the sorcerer's plans. Could they still be under Balin's mind-control?

Eral's gaze rested on Taurus. "Round up those living or wounded. Karny, take one of Balin's horses and head to Lord Kir's realm and request permission to bring our prisoners to Emerald City."

He heard Kalina release a tight breath. When he turned to face her the look of approval that sparkled in her eyes was all he needed to see to know he made the right decision.

She placed a gentle hand on his arm. "You will need to place them in a chamber where Balin's mind powers cannot control them. When the sorcerer is finally vanquished, perhaps they can be freed to live normal lives once again."

Karny gave a quick grin. "She will make a fine queen. You are going to have your hands full with that one."

"I have no doubt on both accounts." Eral took Kalina into his embrace. He pressed his lips to her forehead and squeezed her tightly. "No doubt at all, my love."

Chapter Fourteen

ℬ

Eral had just called her *my love.*

And had she really told him she loved him earlier?

Eral reached up to stroke her black hair from her face, his touch feather-soft against her skin. "Yes, you told me you loved me, just as I love you. We were meant for one another."

"But werefin and weretiger…" What had she been thinking? And what about Mikaela? How could she let her friend face the future alone?

"We will work it out." He took her hand in his and this time she let him. "For now we must head to Lord Kir's realm."

Horses were taken from Balin's stables to carry both black-robed *bakir* prisoners and Eral's warriors. Common folk who lived in the village within the castle baileys remained hidden from sight, as if they feared for their lives. >From Balin or the werefins and dragon, Kalina was not sure. Perhaps from them all. Her heart ached for the people but she knew there was no possible way their entourage could take an entire village with them. The time would come when Balin would be defeated and all peoples of Malachad would be set free.

Bakirs and werefins rode on horseback, but Kalina chose to run in her weretiger form. Eral had ordered her to ride with him when she told him her plans, but she simply shifted and bounded ahead through the castle walls and into the thick of the forest. She heard Eral's curse behind her and the clomp of his horse's hooves as he hurried to catch up.

As if he could reach her. She snorted then gave a satisfied roar and stretched her legs as she ran through the forest.

The exhilaration of the run set her senses free. This time she was not taken unaware by her feelings of freedom. She was keenly aware of her surroundings, rather than blinded as she had been when she was captured by Balin. She had been a fool earlier. After so much time underwater, she had let herself run without care.

Scents of earth, pine and wildlife filled her nostrils and she gave another roar of pleasure. Loam was soft beneath her paws and she easily bounded over any felled trees in her path. Branches and leaves brushed her coat and the wind felt incredible against her face, flattening her ears and the hair on her head. Behind her came the sound of horses' hooves and the occasional word spoken from one werefin to another.

Could she ever give this up to live with Eral in Atlantis?

She sensed Eral's anger with her for disobeying his order that she remain with him, but she cared not. A swell of pleasure spread through her body. Perhaps he would punish her in some delightful way once they were alone.

She heard a now familiar buzzing sound ahead and came to a stop, then began to walk along a log with feline grace. In moments Lacos was zipping around her head.

Kalina, the tiny sea dragon said in her mind as he hovered in front of her face. *You should not run alone, no you should not. The woods are dangerous. Yes they are.* His head snapped to the left and right as if he expected something to jump out from behind the trees.

She resisted batting at the creature between her paws just for the joy of playing — and for his comment. She ignored his remark and responded to him in mind-speak. *What news do you have, friend?*

The man Steele — he is human no more. Lacos looked beyond agitated. *A fearsome creature he is. And powers — somehow he has obtained magic from the sorceress who turned him into the great octopus.*

169

Kalina bounded off the log she had been perched on and sat back on her haunches on leaves and soft earth. Her heart pounded as she considered Lacos' words. *That is dark magic the sorceress performed. Changing another's form is forbidden.*

The pregnant Queen of Clubs and her king would be in more danger than before—and likely they were not aware of Steele's transformation. She knew that the kings of Clubs and Spades searched even now for the evil man who had escaped their grasp before Lord Kir had bonded with Lady Abby.

Kalina gave a low, rumbling growl. *Where is the bastard now?* she asked, but then caught the whiff of something on the wind—man. She raised her nose and inhaled. A man, yet not a man. And it was no weretiger, werewolf or werefin. Whatever it was, it was not entirely human.

Smell him? Yes. Yes, you do. Lacos turned to the left of her where she had caught the scent. His tiny wings were a blur. *He is not far, sorceress. Not far indeed.* Nervously, he fluttered back and forth in front of her face. *Must go back. Find King Eral before the beast catches your scent as well. Go back. Go back.*

Behind her the thud of horses' hooves and the swoosh of branches as the animals passed through became louder to her sensitive tiger ears. *Inform King Eral,* she said, *while I scout out this* thing.

Fear flashed across Lacos' tiny face. *No. No! Do not go alone. Kill me, yes the king will, and you put yourself in danger. Must turn back. Turn back now.*

Kalina could not help batting her paw at the sea dragon, but with no intention of hitting him. *Go. I will not approach this creature once known as Steele. You have my word that I will merely seek him out and wait for King Eral's arrival. I will not let the beast see me.*

But—

Her eyes met his. *Steele is a creature of magic. I, as the only sorceress present, have a duty to the world and the king to try and anticipate and counter what dark or wild magic the thing might*

170

possess. Her mental voice softened. *I promise, the beast will be unaware of my presence as I wait for King Eral.*

The dragon gave another agitated buzz of his wings as he dodged her paw. *The Kings of Clubs and Spades must be west of Steele, as well as werewolves. When I was near the creature, caught weretiger and werewolf scent, I did.* He twitched his muzzle, his nostrils flaring.

Kalina raised her nose to the wind, but the musk of weretigers and werewolves was not yet on the breeze. *I will seek them out.* She glanced back to Lacos. *Hurry and inform King Eral.*

Be careful, Lacos said before zipping away toward the direction Eral was coming from. He was close. She caught his unique male scent and sensed his anger at not being able to catch up with her.

Yes, her punishment would be especially harsh, indeed. The thought would have made her laugh if she were not in her weretiger form. Instead she gave a low rumbling purr that quickly turned into a growl as she changed direction and began to hunt the creature known as Steele.

On silent paws she stealthily made her way through the forest. It was not long before her keen hearing caught Steele's movements and his smell became stronger as she neared him. His odor was part human, part beast, and also carried the briny smell of the ocean. Could Steele now be of both the earth and the sea?

She also scented werewolves and weretigers, but heard nothing as they slowly stalked Steele. The other were-beings were to the west of the beast, whereas she was to the east.

Unless Steele now had the hearing and sense of smell of a were-creature, he could not possibly know she was near.

Every muscle in her finely tuned body tightened as she neared Steele. She heard nothing for a moment. He was not moving—it was as if he were waiting. But then the squeal of a rabbit met her ears immediately followed by the crunch of bones and the smell of blood.

She crept forward until she finally saw Steele.

He was eating a rabbit, fur and all. Blood dribbled down his chin, and when he finished devouring the creature, he wiped his mouth, smearing blood across his face and on his hand. Even though were-beings naturally preyed on creatures for fresh meat, she could not help a shudder at the sight of Steele devouring the rabbit.

But that was not what truly caught her attention—it was the man/not a man, himself. The naked beast had expanded in girth to that of three men and had grown to be at least ten feet tall. His skin was as gray as that of an octopus. His head was bald, his eyes bulged, his penis was thick, large and malformed, and his bloody lips were a slash of a cruel grin across his face.

And he had four arms. Four powerful, muscular arms.

Kalina's tail twitched back and forth as she crouched low. The beast had magic—powerful magic. As a sorceress she could feel it in every fiber of her being.

Behind her she heard the virtually silent approach of Eral and his men as she caught their scents. They no longer rode on horseback—she did not smell horse, nor hear sounds they would have made through the forest.

She did not move a muscle as Eral settled his hand on her back and peeked through the same opening she was using to spy on Steele, but she sensed his displeasure with her. In his other hand he held his crossbow already loaded with a deadly arrow. His body was tense and his jaw set as he looked upon the creature. Hatred rolled off his skin in waves that thickened the air. Kalina also sensed Eral's men directly behind her.

Lacos, now in his smaller form, silently landed on Eral's shoulder. *Told you, I did*, the dragon said in mind-speak.

Steele cocked his head as if listening to something then raised his nose to the sky.

Could Steele now hear mind-speak?

Kalina and Eral both glanced at Lacos with narrowed eyes, telling him without words to be quiet. The dragon looked chagrined and said nothing more.

As Steele slowly moved his massive head to look around the clearing, Kalina's sorceress' senses told her that Steele heard the dragon's mind-speak. When he sniffed loudly, she realized her fears must be true—Steele's sense of smell was enhanced as well.

Eral glanced at Lacos again and gave a slight nod. The tiny sea dragon rose into the air and immediately zipped through the forest, heading southwest, skirting Steele's location. Instinctively she knew he was going to the weretigers and werewolves on the other side of the clearing to let them know they were not alone. Likely they were already aware due to the weretiger and werefin scents, but they needed to be assured. How Lacos would do it without mind-speak, Kalina was not sure. Perhaps with some kind of sign language. The weretigers and werewolves would no doubt be surprised by the sight of a tiny flying dragon.

Steele started moving in a circle, sniffing the air. He clenched his mighty fists, all four of them and gave a hideous growl.

Eral buried his own fist in Kalina's fur, as if warning her not to involve herself in the attack, but she merely shook off his hold and crouched, prepared to spring at the beast in the center of the clearing.

Kalina had no intention of holding back. Her emotions and her magic had been set free by Eral, and anger burned deep within her at the thought of what this being had done as a human.

Steele continued circling the clearing.

When he neared her, Steele's gaze riveted on the location where Kalina crouched.

Hair rose on her body, her skin prickled and her tail twitched with menace.

Eral tensed beside her and raised his crossbow.

Steele charged, his bellow reverberating throughout the clearing and forest.

Eral loosed the arrow from his bow.

With a roar Kalina sprang from her hiding place, straight for the bastard. Her jaws prepared to rip into the thick vein on the inside of his leg.

Steele expanded his four arms at the same time Kalina sprang forward and Eral released his arrow.

The sorceress slammed into a barrier just as Eral's arrow bounced off the same barrier. The power of her leap and the force of the invisible wall flung Kalina into the trees. She gave a wild scream as her head rammed into the trunk of a massive pine. Sparks flashed in her mind.

The gates of hell broke open.

Werewolves and weretigers sprang from their hiding places, all with snapping jaws, foaming mouths and death in their eyes—intent on killing Steele. Werefins in their male forms also burst from the treeline, swords swinging, knives held in fists, and bows strung taut.

Every were-creature bounced off the shield surrounding Steele, and every were-creature charged again, never giving up.

Kalina shook the sparks from her head and stumbled to her feet. Her vision crossed then cleared.

She knew what she had to do.

The sorceress shifted into her human form. White and black hair slipped back through her pores, her face grew smaller, her front legs lengthened into arms, and her hindquarters changed to ass and long human legs. She straightened her naked form, raised her chin and narrowed her eyes. She stepped forward toward the giant man who was able to fling away the were-creatures, with his shield still up.

But that shield was failing.

The weretigers and werewolves never stopped their attack. The werefins continued to hack at the barrier with swords, knives and arrows, aiming for the beast's head, obviously careful not to hurt their fellow were-creatures. Every blow appeared to weaken the barrier.

Howls, roars and cat screams rent the air. Steele bellowed, a wild light of pleasure in his eyes as his four arms flung away his attackers. His shield did not hold him back from attacking, only from being attacked.

She took another step forward.

"No, Kalina!" she heard Eral shout from where he now fought across the clearing when she walked from the treeline.

She kept her focus on Steele. Raised her hands. Palms facing the beast.

Steele's gaze riveted on her and he charged.

Kalina stood her ground even as Steele neared her. Her long black hair rose from her shoulders. Her skin burned and prickled from her scalp to her face, to the soles of her feet.

With all the power she'd tamped down over countless years, power that had been freed in the cave of sponges, and even more so in Balin's castle, she let loose a burst of magic.

The magic was filled with rage at the loss of so many lives in Incasha, the life of Eral's brother, and what Steele had done to Awai.

Kalina's power slammed into Steele just as he reached out to grab her.

His eyes bulged with terror as he stumbled back. His shield shimmered and a crack like the sound of thunder filled the air.

She destroyed his protections with a single blast.

Immediately weretigers and werewolves brought Steele to his knees. But it was a great white-and-black-striped tiger with a club tattoo that slammed Steele onto his back.

Ty! The King of Clubs!

The power of Ty's forelegs brought the beast down, the weretiger's forepaws planted firmly on the four-armed creature's chest. With a growl that shook the forest, Ty opened his massive jaws and ripped Steele's throat out.

Blood bubbled up from Steele's neck as he screamed, but Ty did not stop. The weretiger took the man-beast by the neck, shook his head violently back and forth, and severed Steele's head from his body.

Only then did Ty raise his bloodied muzzle to the sky to give another roar, this time one of revenge for his mate, Awai, the Queen of Clubs. Steele would never abuse or harm another being again.

After transforming into her weretiger form and back again, Kalina was rejuvenated and high on bloodlust.

She now rode on horseback with Eral behind her, his arm tight around her waist. Lacos perched on Eral's shoulder, his incessant chatter enough to drive the most patient of persons out of their minds. She managed a smile as the horses continued to Oz. She would not have the little beast any other way.

Kir had fought as a werewolf alongside his were-brethren. He now loped ahead toward his Emerald City. After Steele's death, he had agreed to keep the captive *bakirs* within his realm, but this time far, far below the surface of the ground with the most powerful of magic to block Balin from using his mind-control to summon them once again.

They followed Kir down the Yellow Road and through the great gates that led to Emerald City, Eral's leather breeches and his rigid cock chafing Kalina's naked ass with every step the horse made. Eral's chest brushed her bare back and her quim rubbed against the saddle, causing her nipples to remain hard, her folds wet. Several times she thought she would climax from all the incredible sensations. Eral was quiet as they rode and she was certain his concern for her during the battle bothered him still.

When he swung from their mount at the golden gates, Eral helped her down. Lacos still perched on Eral's shoulder.

Lacos buzzed his wings. "Go, I must, back to the sea. I have been gone far too long, yes I have."

Kalina reached up and with one finger stroked the tiny dragon's forehead then placed her lips on his head, giving him a light kiss before she drew back. "I cannot thank you enough for all that you have done for us."

If dragons could blush, she was certain Lacos did. She could swear his bluish-green cheeks tinged with red.

"Thank you, my friend," Eral said, his voice serious. "I will see you soon, yes?"

Lacos gave a nod of his little head. "Yes, yes you will."

The other werefins gave him cheeky farewells with lots of teasing, but great appreciation in their voices. With one more zip around them all, he took off toward the sea.

Eral stepped away from her and exchanged words with Kir that she couldn't quite discern at the same time she watched Lacos fly away. He quickly turned into a tiny speck and then was gone. When she looked back to the two men she saw Lord Kir glance at her before looking back to Eral and nodding.

Eral returned to where Kalina stood and without a word took her by the hand. She followed, wondering what he had in mind. He guided her into the beautiful underground city. They entered the main cavern, fashioned by nature out of emeralds. They were lit from the glowing lichen that grew around the base of each emerald, much like Atlantis was brightened.

They walked side by side and he finally brought her to a pair of wooden doors. When they stepped into the chamber, Eral closed the doors behind them.

She swallowed, feeling both panic and pleasure at the sight of so many whips, floggers, and other tools of her former lifestyle, including a St. Andrew's cross, a cage, a swing, a hook dangling from the ceiling and so much more.

No words were exchanged as they stood nose to nose. The heat of his eyes burned into her skin as she caressed the tight lines of his face with her gaze. When she inhaled her breath hitched.

In that moment of silence, Kalina realized what she had discovered on this journey with Eral.

How very much she loved him.

But there was more.

Her pulse raced, her body warmed with anticipation of being dominated by Eral. Where before she had enjoyed the rule of the Tarok kings, her freedom had given her a taste of independence, something she had refused to surrender, until now.

She wanted everything from Eral. His love and even his mastery, but only inside the bedroom—or dungeon.

His blue eyes never leaving hers, he took a step forward, crowding her so that she felt the heat of his body. She allowed a smile to flicker across her face as with one step after another he guided her backward until she bumped into a wall, her palms flat against the cool stone surface. His nostrils flared and she swore she smelled the salty ocean rise from his flesh.

"You could have been killed." His voice was low, gravelly, as he captured her lips in a kiss that took her breath away. There was both tenderness and a savage hunger in the way they came together. "You should be punished, my little witch," he said when he drew away. "Do you not agree?"

"Yes, Master." Kalina gave a soft moan. The word *Master* came easily to her. That's what she wanted from this man right now. His mastery over her.

"Do you know what it is I should punish you for?" he asked as he nibbled at her collarbone.

The ache between her thighs made her squirm. "I disobeyed you, Master."

Eral raised his head and braced his palms on the wall to either side of her head and studied her. "I know you have relished your freedom. Do you wish to relinquish that power to me?"

Her heart pounded as she slowly nodded. "But," she licked her lips, "in the bedroom. Times when we are alone...Master."

He studied her for a moment and she saw a spark in his eyes. A spark of pleasure or pride, or both. "What is your safe word, my little witch?"

She thought for a moment then gave him a teasing grin. "Bubbles."

Eral shook his head and laughed. "Bubbles indeed."

Chapter Fifteen

ℬ

"I must punish you now, witch," he said and she nodded, a hint of a smile on her lips.

Eral pinned her against the cave wall of the emerald cavern they had entered and immediately took her mouth again in a rough kiss. He moved back and forth across her softness. She melted against him and her surrender was sweet. Blood filled his sac and rushed down his cock, hardening it to a painful ache as he ground his leather-clad body against her naked one. His assault on Kalina's lips and body was a result of the fear trapped inside him fighting to be released. Once again she had defied him and placed herself in danger.

Memories of the last time they made love and the ripple of colors beneath her skin quickly morphing to black was all he could see.

Death.

Her death or that of another at her hands.

Just the thought made his nerve endings sizzle with fear. His breathing was ragged, filled with anxiety tightly leashed during the long ride to Lord Kir's realm. He plunged his tongue into her mouth. Pain shook the roots of his teeth as they met hers in the passionate exchange.

He had lost his brother. He refused to lose her too.

When she had faced the beast known as Steele, Eral's blood had gone cold. For a second all he could think of was living without her. Pressure built in his chest again, as he realized how close he had been to never feeling her arms around him, tasting her lips, nor basking in the warmth of her body against his. The thought nearly suffocated him.

With one hand wrapped around her wrists, high above her head, he pulled so that she rose onto the tips of her toes. He tested her limits, legs and arms straining tight, so that she was completely in his control. He alone held her centered as he pried her thighs apart with his knee.

As he devoured her mouth, he thrust a finger into her wet quim. The cry she released against his mouth only fired his desire. Her nipples were hard beads pressing into his vest.

Damn his clothing.

Her hips pressed against his hand as he drove in and out of her warmth. She was tight, so very wet and ready for him to take her. But in their play, she no doubt knew that one's pleasure was not always given without merit.

The damn woman had scared the shit out of him.

He broke the kiss and barely stopped himself from shaking her. Before they went any further the time for honesty had come. "Kalina, I acknowledge the strength of your magic." He swallowed hard. Godsdamn, this was hard to admit. He mentally pushed aside his pride, as his finger rested quietly inside her. "That you do not need me to take care of you — protect you. That should you stay with me it is of your own free will." He realized the chance he took in acknowledging her independence, the rights she had not only as a magnificent sorceress, but as a woman — his mate and queen.

Eral could not miss the twinkle in her eyes, nor the way they grew misty.

He let out a breath of exasperation. "Gods, woman, can you not see it is not my nature to allow my mate to run freely into danger?" His voice softened, the lump in his throat thickened. "I could have lost you today." He trembled with the thought. Her expression was tender as she gazed into his eyes. "I am the King of Atlantis." For the first time since he had taken the throne a sense of pride washed over him. "Understand that to question my judgment, to run into danger against my wishes, diminishes my authority. I cannot allow it."

"I do understand. But I am a sorceress. My visions call to me and I must obey." Confidence was both in her expression and the rigidness of her spine.

"My little witch, I know this is true." He smiled softly. "But you must allow me the illusion that I rule you." He pressed his lips to the tip of her nose. "Can you do that?"

She nodded, but he wondered how long her resignation would last, as his fingers began to push in and out of her wetness again. Her hips responded in turn, thrusting against his hand.

With his thumb he applied pressure against her clit. A tremor assailed her, shimmering through her and then him. She gasped as another of his fingers bathed in her heat. Her mouth parted on a gasp as she began to writhe against him. Light from the lichen-covered gems caressed her features with a soft green glow. Her eyes were dark with desire.

"Let me touch you." It was a breathy plea that Eral ignored as he held her immobile by her wrists and kept the pressure of his body against hers.

"You will not speak. Not one word." He did not trust himself when he felt this much emotion. He could have lost her today. The breath he sucked in between clenched teeth he released slowly, easing the glide of his hand between her thighs. *Control.* He trembled attempting to grasp the elusive concept.

When he withdrew his fingers from her body, she whimpered. The cry stroked his ears like silk dragging seductively across them and he shivered.

She wanted him. Needed to feel his cock buried inside her body. The evidence was written in the heaviness of her breathing, the way her tongue slid across her bottom lip and the creaminess between her thighs.

Fire burned behind his eyes as his emotions spiraled, churning inside him like currents moving in different directions beneath a calm surface. He loved this woman. She was of the Tarok kingdom, soon to be his queen. She must learn to live as she was born to. "You will be punished for disobeying me."

"Yes, Master." Her quick response left him momentarily speechless. All he could do was gaze into the amber depths of her eyes. There was something conflicting in her words and the way she refused to drop her head in a subservient manner. Then she winked and his aplomb nearly fell apart.

The little witch was looking forward to being punished.

Kalina was going to be the death of him. She had changed so very much from when they first met. The calm, collected sorceress was gone. A much stronger, feistier woman stood in her place. He did not know whether to be infuriated with her or simply give her what she wanted. He released her wrists and reached for each of her nipples, grasped them tightly between his fingers and twisted. He watched the tendons in her throat work as she swallowed hard. The corners of her mouth twitched, giving away her excitement.

There would be no lesson in obedience with Kalina. She enjoyed the role too much. It was as Lord Kir had once told him — she was born to be a submissive.

Then fine! He would test her limits for both their pleasures.

He squeezed her nipples harder, as he mentally called from the sea his nipple teasers. The two matching starfish that he had placed once before on her breasts appeared, hovering in the air with a thread of green seaweed intertwined between them. Again her lips twitched as she fought to hide her joy at seeing the two animals.

One last sharp pinch brought a gasp from her full lips. He released her and reached for the starfish. Peeling the seaweed off, he tossed it aside then centered the spiny fish over each nipple. As the suction took hold she closed her eyes and arched her back. He could not help splaying his hands over each breast, feeling their heaviness as he massaged gently.

The truth was he loved sexual play when both parties received satisfaction simultaneously. He could not wait to see his mark on her ass, hear her scream for completion and listen to her cries of ecstasy as his colors rippled through her body. His chest tightened. The breath he attempted was strangled.

Godsdamn this thing called love. The emotion was enough to bring a warrior to his knees. Or turn them to the same substance of a jellyfish, because that was exactly how Eral's knees were feeling at the moment.

He needed Kalina to the point of obsession. He knew their differences would not be easy to overcome. But by the heavens above he would find a way for them to be together.

The cavern that Eral had asked Lord Kir for the use of was the werewolf's playroom. It had every imaginable sex toy a man could want, but werefins had their own unique blend of toys, like the starfish. Eral preferred the salty scent of seaweed to ropes for binding and he had a special toy in mind for Kalina.

"Follow me." Eral led the way to a rock carved into a spanking bench with a step and O-rings attached at each corner. For her disobedience she would feel the sting of his hand. The bench was covered in rich, thick furs, which would protect Kalina's tender skin from the rough surface below. Additional furs lay upon the ground. "Kneel on the step and lay flat on the stone's surface."

"Yes, Master." The bench was the perfect height so that when she lay on her stomach, her ass was completely exposed. The scrapes and bruises that Balin had inflicted had vanished when she had transformed into a tiger.

He was in awe of the beautiful woman stretched out before him. Godsdamn, she had a gorgeous ass.

Eral could not help reaching out and cupping the rounded globes. With his finger he traced the swollen folds of her quim so, so very wet with her arousal. As he pinched her clit, he felt the shiver that raced through her.

Again Eral called to the ocean for several items that appeared in his palms, all wrapped in a large wad of seaweed and red algae. He stepped away from Kalina and laid the items on a small rock table next to the bench.

He stripped several vines of kelp from the table and came to stand before Kalina. "You have been a very bad witch," he chastised as he began to bind each wrist to an O-ring. "For that you must be punished."

"Yes, Master." Her cheek lay against the soft furs and she parted her mouth invitingly. Her long black hair draped across her back and tumbled over the sides of the table. He moved beside her and brushed aside her tresses, exposing her back. Slowly he ran the wet, cool seaweed down her spine. She squirmed beneath his tender assault.

Then Eral moved behind her to admire her ass. "Part your knees for me." As she did, he was gifted with the glistening of her arousal, wet upon the hairless folds of her quim. His pulse jumped with desire to taste her, to run his tongue across her mons and delve into her warmth. But that would have to wait, he thought as he began to bind her ankles with seaweed to the O-rings situated on the ends of the step.

He ran his warm palm over the cool skin of one of Kalina's ass cheeks. She was beautiful, strapped and spread wide for his pleasure. "My little witch, tell me why I must spank you." He dipped a finger in the crevice that parted her beautiful ass.

Chin resting on the bench, her gaze away from him, she said, "Because your wishes were not followed."

He reached for a shell from the table and pushed his finger into the silky contents. As he rubbed the gel over the outside of her puckered rosebud, he added, "And?"

185

Her back rose with each breath. She turned her head so the other side of her face rested on the bench's fur-covered surface again. "And because I placed myself in danger against your orders."

His finger pushed beyond the tight entrance, working the gel deeper into her body. In and out. In and out. She strained against the bindings at her wrists and pushed her ass against his hand.

Gods, he loved how tight she was.

When he extracted his finger she whimpered lightly. Her eyelashes were dark crescents on her cheeks. Her lips were parted as she breathed deeply.

From the table he chose a very special, much-coveted sea cucumber that was known only to the people of Atlantis. The long brown animal moved in his palm and then stiffened. Its thick rubbery spines were slightly retracted from its body, small nubs over its slick skin. The creature would lengthen and shorten its tentacles at Eral's command. Another ability it possessed was to throw out its internal body parts making it bigger, thicker at will. Not to mention its respiratory tree would release puffs of air adding to her sensations.

Standing behind Kalina once more, he held the sea cucumber to her rosebud and pushed. As it slid inside, disappearing from his sight, she gasped and caught her breath in a surprised sound. It was followed by a moan as he mind-spoke to the creature to release its spines. Each tentacle had suction disks on their ends that allowed it to move freely, enhancing what she would feel. Kalina squirmed and cried out at what he knew must be sensations she had never experienced before.

He began to stroke each cheek of her ass, warming her skin and awakening the nerve endings. His hand snapped against her tender skin causing her to jerk against her seaweed bindings. The result was a large pink handprint. He rubbed the spot quickly bringing the blood to the surface before he struck her on the other ass cheek. Spanking her with one handprint over the other, he reveled in her pink skin tone, even the sweet sting in his hand. The entire time she squirmed from the sea cucumber and the sensations it must be causing within her.

Placing the cheek of his face against her ass he felt the burn. Then he turned and nipped her.

She squealed. The tight high-pitched sound made him grin.

"How should I punish you, witch?"

"However would please you, *Master*." Her last word caught in her throat when he ordered the sea cucumber to move. She shifted, her red bottom squirming. "But please do it quickly."

As he watched her rosebud pulse from the action inside her, his cock swelled. The pressure was hard against his leather pants, needing to be released.

He was suffocating in all these clothes.

Leaning against the rock table beside the spanking bench, he bent and pulled off one boot after the other, instead of magically removing them. He wanted to draw out her need for him. Through half-shuttered eyelids she watched him undress. As he pulled off the vest her eyes widened. Her tongue once again slid across her bottom lip. The small movement made him focus on her mouth. The pain between his thighs made him think of what that mouth could do to ease his suffering. The ties slid between his fingers. Just thinking about her lips wrapped around him sent a ray of fire down his shaft. After slowly removing his clothing, he stood naked in front of her.

"Suck my cock, witch." He moved closer and she flicked her tongue across his crown. He squeezed a breath in through clenched teeth. *Godsdamn*. She was warm and wet and willing, as she licked a path up and down his erection. He ground his teeth, waiting breathlessly for the moment she would bury him inside her mouth. Instead she rimmed the head, sliding her tongue across to taste the pearly drop at the small slit.

She was playing with him.

Teasing.

Wanting to see how far she could push him until he cracked like a day-old sea sponge.

"So this is how you want to play the game," he said in a low growl.

She gave a hint of a grin.

He should be angry at her for not obeying him, but he could not. This was what sex was all about. Playful and fun. Stretching the sensation out, enhancing the desire until his body cried out for release.

She would pay for taunting him, he thought with a smile on his lips. But not now. He was enjoying her whimsical mood.

He slipped his fingers through her silky hair then held her head firmly and thrust his hips forward. His cock met closed lips. He stepped back and raised a brow in warning.

A spark twinkled in her eyes. Her expression softened, as she slowly began to open her mouth. She flicked her tongue, inviting him in.

He moved forward, careful not to stumble over his feet in his haste. The muscles in his throat worked as he swallowed hard and held his breath. Then she closed her mouth around him and he was lost. The sensation was like falling off a cliff. He shuttered his eyelids. There was nothing to anchor him as he tumbled headfirst into the heavens. The pounding of his heart echoed in his ears. Her mouth was so wet. The pull against his groin made him tighten his hold on her hair. Soft mewling sounds slipped from her mouth as she sucked him hard and brought him deep to the back of her throat.

"Kalina." Her name was a whisper on his lips. "My witch. My lovely witch."

When his balls drew tight against his body, the bittersweet ache made him open his eyes. Kalina looked beautiful bound by seaweed to the spanking bench. In her semi-kneeling position her ass was raised high, her thighs spread wide. Yet the headiest sight was his cock moving in and out of her precious mouth. Her expression of arousal, intense and enduring as she took him deep sent shivers one after another through him. He was only holding on by a sliver of kelp.

He tensed, easing her head back and released his cock from her mouth. Looking down upon her, he said, "My turn."

An array of emotions raced across her face. Excitement. Fear. Anticipation. He loved watching them flicker in her eyes.

From the table he unwound two seaweed floggers. They were still wet and slick from the ocean as his fingers curled around the shafts and he held one in each hand. Lightly he dragged the cool ends across her ass that still sported a bright hue. Then he began to flick his wrist. The rhythm was slow at first, building until the flogger hummed through the air. At the same time he used mind-speak, commanding the sea cucumber to move and enlarge.

Once again, Kalina turned her face so that her cheek rested on the fur-covered bench. From this position he could see her expressions. The small *O* her mouth formed as she regulated her breathing. The taut lines that creased her forehead let him know he struck a rather sensitive area.

Then he reversed the action so that the tips of the floggers nipped at the sweet spot where her ass met her thighs. The minute the first thongs touched the crease she began to shake. "Eral, I'm going to come." There was a cry of desperation in her voice. She even forgot to refer to him as Master as her restraint begin to slip.

He eased his swing. "Hold, witch. I have yet to give you permission, and you failed to call me Master."

By the way she tightened her buttocks, the uncontrollable tremor, he knew she was barely able to contain her climax.

He was not doing much better.

His erection was rock-hard and arched to where it nearly touched his navel. He had to widen his stance to give his tender balls enough room so that as he swung the flogger the strands did not come in contact with his thighs.

It was hell—pure hell.

With a flick of his wrists he tossed the floggers over his shoulders. He moved forward and placed his cock between her swollen folds.

He had to have her. Had to be deep inside her.

But no...he had to make her wait. Wait. Wait.

Gods, it was killing him.

Eral teased her quim with his erection. "Do you want my cock, witch?"

She moaned. "Yes, Master. *Please.*"

He rubbed his cock hard against her clit and it was all he could do to rein in his control. He swore he started to see stars, and ground his teeth.

Gods above, he could not take it anymore.

Eral thrust forward.

He buried his throbbing erection deep inside her.

Kalina gasped and cried out. Eral groaned.

For a moment, he held perfectly still and let the sensations of their joining set in. She was wet and warm around him. Her cave palpitated, squeezing him. Her fists were clenched, her expression tense, as she released a shuddering breath.

With his mind-speak, he commanded the sea cucumber to stretch within her ass.

Kalina squirmed and her features twisted into a tortured expression. "Oh, gods. I must come, Master. Please!"

"No, witch. Not until I give you permission." He took time to calm the beast within him that wanted to be released. Then he began to move, pumping in and out of her slowly, enjoying the soft cries she made with every thrust.

Gods, he loved this woman. Never would he get enough of taking her body. Now if she would only give him her soul.

His fingers pressed into her hips as he increased the rhythm. The sound of flesh slapping flesh, the knowledge of the sea cucumber buried in her ass and the scent of their lovemaking, nearly undid Eral. But it was not enough. He needed to see her expression, the wildness in her eyes when she came.

With just a thought the seaweed around her wrists and ankles disappeared, as well as the sea cucumber inside her. She gave a cry and shuddered when the cucumber vanished from her taut ass.

The bundle of other sea items he had called forth disappeared as well. Slowly he slid his cock from her body. "Get up, witch." Now that she was no longer bound, he helped her to stand. "Lay down on the fur next to the bench." Her cheeks were flushed, her amber eyes dark with arousal, and her black hair tousled around her shoulders as she lay upon her back. He kneeled down at her feet, feeling the softness beneath his legs. Her fingers flexed and for a moment he thought she would touch him. "Spread your thighs."

His eyes riveted on her mons as she bared herself. He slipped between her thighs, and brought their bodies together once more. His cock nudged her opening, and she shifted to give him better access. In one swift movement he entered her.

"You feel so good. Gods, I could remain buried within you forever." The words just slipped out of his mouth. But he meant every one of them. He had never felt this way with another woman.

She leaned upward and wrapped her arms around his neck. "Could you?"

He grinned. "You sassy witch. You know I enjoy fucking you."

She gave him a coy look through heavy lashes. "How much?"

"Let me show you." He growled as he looped his arms beneath her thighs spreading her wider.

The action threw her off balance. Her arms came from around his neck, jerking behind her so that she leaned back on her palms for support.

He could not take much more. He began to fuck her hard and fast. Their bodies pounded together. Their breathing grew even more labored.

"Master?" she cried.

"Yes, witch. Come for me." He fell forward, pushing her back against the fur as his body covered hers.

Who screamed first, Eral had no idea. But their voices lifted as they tumbled over the precipice as one.

Fingernails dug into his back as they rocked back and forth. The sweet pain did not come close to the pressure ripping through his cock as he filled Kalina with his hot seed. His cock jerked several times, while her body squeezed him tight. Ripple after ripple, her body tensed and then released to milk him dry of both come and energy.

With growing tension he watched the colors of her orgasm flow over her. Red...orange...yellow...green...blue...and brilliant white. No purple. No black.

But white!

Relief warmed him, his mind free of what danger her future might hold.

"Thank the gods," he murmured without thought.

Kalina gave a soft laugh beneath him. "For what?"

He braced himself with his palms against the fur and rose so that he could gaze into her eyes. He made no attempt to conceal the concern he had felt. "When we made love before...I saw the colors of purple and black in your orgasm." He gave a smile at the relief he felt. "But not this time. It is gone."

She frowned. "Purple and black? What do those colors mean?"

Eral debated on telling her the truth, but knew that he owed her truth in every aspect. "They mean death...yours, or by your hand." His smile returned. "But the colors—they are gone."

Tears trickled from Kalina's eyes and her expression grew tortured. "Letta. The sorceress. I caused her death." She sniffed loudly and gave a shuddering sigh. "I did not mean to. I tried to catch her before she fell...but the force of my magic caused her to tumble from the window of the tower to her death on the rocks below."

"Oh, my love." Eral wrapped his arms around her as she sobbed against his chest. "You did not harm her intentionally. It was not your fault—you have the right to defend yourself."

"But...but..." She hiccupped between her sobs. "You even saw...saw death by my hand in the colors."

Eral stroked her hair as he held her and felt her warm tears against his chest. "They did not mean you intentionally caused death. It was not your fault. The colors show that. Especially since I saw white this time. White is pure—if you were not pure of heart, it would not be there."

She sniffed again, but he felt her relax in his arms. Their hearts and breathing matched. It was peaceful. It was perfect.

After a few moments, he stood, lifting her into his arms, taking the fur beneath her as he carried her to a corner of the room. Gently he laid her down, fur and all, following her, so that they lay side to side. She curled into him, releasing a sigh.

"Now perhaps you will tell me more about this surprising power you've kept hidden?" He gently stroked her cheek. "You know about me, my family history. I know none of yours."

Kalina sighed. "I never knew my parents—I was taken from them as a cub by an old witch. I heard later that my parents had been murdered."

Eral gently stroked Kalina's cheek, saying nothing, letting her take the lead in how much she would tell him.

Her amber eyes focused on his. "The witch who took me from my parents wanted to exploit my growing powers." Kalina's jaw tensed. "I held them inside me, refused to give in. No matter how many times the woman beat me, I thwarted her. Finally, when I was eighteen the witch took me from the Realm of the Trees, where I grew up."

At that Eral stilled. "You are from the Realm of Trees?" He knew it was purported to be a place with great magical families who could trace their lineage for centuries.

Kalina sighed. "Yes. And I was sold into slavery in Tarok."

"*What?*" Eral could not help the fury from his voice. "I have never heard of slavery being tolerated by any of the kings."

"It was not—is not." She took a deep breath. "I was sold to an underground slavery ring, but fortunately King Jarronn took me from my captors and set me free. I chose to serve as seer to the four Tarok kings until they were all mated."

Eral forced down the fury he felt at the thought of what his beautiful sorceress had been through when she was so young, but he was certain it was in his eyes, in his expression.

Kalina gave a gentle smile and this time she brushed her hand over his cheek. "It was a long time ago. I had been happy with my life for countless years." She turned her head slightly and her last words held weight.

I had *been happy with my life for countless years.*

What did she mean by *had*?

Of course. Their differences.

His gut churned. He did not want to think of the future at the moment. He did not want to address the problems between their different lifestyles. So when Kalina asked, "How am I to live without you?" the question rocked him to his core and he couldn't speak. It took a moment for him to understand that although she had professed her love, she had no intentions of being his queen.

"You will not live without me, as I will not live without you." There, he said it. No more needed to be said. They would work the issues out later.

Kalina released a breath of obvious disbelief. "Eral, we cannot fight the fact that you are of the water, and I am of the land."

"There is no need for a fight. What will be will be. We will join and you will become mine."

Kalina pushed out of his arms and rose so that she stared down upon him. "What?"

Eral caressed her cheek with the back of his hand. "Kalina. My sweet witch. Whatever our differences are we will find a way around them."

"But—"

He placed his finger against her lips. A huge knot formed in his throat. "I cannot live without you." The words felt like they were torn from his throat. "If you cannot live and rule beside me in Atlantis then I will denounce my throne to Derel and live with you. Just say that you will be my mate."

Her eyes widened. Before she could speak he said, "Join with me, Kalina."

She was quiet for longer than was comfortable. A single tear slipped from her misty eyes. She cupped his face in her hands and kissed him lightly on the lips. Her mouth parted as if she would say something, and then shut. Several more tears chased each other down her cheeks.

Eral's gut clenched. These were all signs of goodbye.

No! His soul screamed. *No!*

Kalina sniffled. Her voice was filled with emotion when she spoke. "You cannot give up your throne for me."

"How could I not? You are everything to me." He cupped her cheek and wiped a tear from her eye with his thumb. It would kill him to give up his throne, to disappoint not only his family, but his people. Yet he saw no other choice.

She bit down on her bottom lip. Her tear-spiked eyelashes rose as her eyes met his again. "Eral—"

"No. Just say you will join with me." Tension tightened every muscle and tendon in his body. He felt like a stretched piece of twine held too tautly as he awaited her response.

The release was incredible when she nodded. It felt like his insides exploded when she said, "Yes. Oh, gods, I love you." She threw her arms around his neck.

They had jumped one hurdle, Eral thought as he guided her to her back and then slid his body atop hers. "I love you." Pressure built behind his eyes as he entered her body and began to move. His eyelids drifted closed.

He thought of nothing but being inside her, of knowing that she was his forever. The moment he reached climax, Kalina came with him and their cries mingled as one.

When the last pure wave of colors of her orgasm washed over her, he held her close.

Gently he brushed her hair with his hand as he cuddled her, a sadness mixed with the joy of having her to love. "I will tell my people tomorrow that my brother Derel will take my place as King of Atlantis."

"What?" Kalina placed her palm on his chest and pushed herself up so that she was looking down upon him. "You cannot do that. Your people need you."

Confusion mingled with hope. "But you—"

Kalina smiled. "We will compromise. I will live in Atlantis with you, but I will come to the land when I need the freedom to shift into my tiger form and run with the wind, feel the sun upon my face, the exhilaration of being who I am inside."

He rose up so that they were facing one another. "You would do that? Live in Atlantis with me?"

Kalina's Discovery

"Just as you were willing to stay on land for me."

Eral slipped his hand into her hair and brought her to him in a gentle, passionate kiss. "Gods, but I love you, woman," he said as he drew away and stared deep into her amber eyes.

"As I love you." Her smile was brilliant, filled with as much emotion as he felt churning within himself.

He brushed the back of his hand across her cheek. "But I could not allow you to come to land alone. If I cannot join you, you will always have an entourage to ensure your safety. I know you are a powerful sorceress, and studying magic in Atlantis will make your skills even more formidable, but I would worry if you came to land alone. If I cannot join you I will send the Queen's Guard to make extra certain of your safety."

Kalina looked for a moment like she would argue, but then said, "For you, anything, my love."

Chapter Sixteen

ℰↃ

The emotions churning through Kalina were unlike anything she had ever experienced. She had always been calm, collected, serene even.

Not anymore. Eral had freed her.

And now they were to be joined. She would be the Queen of Atlantis. She had always thought her destiny was to serve kings and queens. She never thought nor aspired to be one of them.

Yet here she was. And she was to be married to the man she loved more than anything in either of their worlds.

Kalina looked at her opulent surroundings, the chamber she had shared with Eral since returning to Atlantis. A huge oyster shell bed that shimmered of mother-of-pearl commanded the center of the room. The sheets and bedding were pearl-colored satin and caressed her skin when snuggling deep inside them with her man. Cool air that smelled of seawater circulated through the room, brushing her naked body.

She turned to the smooth, polished walls and studied murals of werefins that graced each surface. The paintings were absolutely breathtaking. She traced the tail of a female werefin on one mural and thought about how surprised she was that she was so comfortable now in Atlantis. She was far below land, deep beneath the sea, and yet she felt no fear of it any longer.

She ran her finger over the bare nipple of the woman in the mural and on up her chest to the curve of her neck. Kalina was pleased with the compromise she and Eral had agreed upon. Whenever she felt the need to be on land, to shift into her tiger form and run with the wind, she would take a transport bubble to the surface for as long as she needed. She shook her head at the next thought though. She would always be accompanied by an entourage who would guard her as Queen of Atlantis. They would ride horseback as she ran as a weretiger through the forests of Lord Kir's realm. At first she had balked at the thought of not being allowed her total freedom, but had given in knowing that as queen she had duties and responsibilities, and that included keeping herself safe and not endangering her people.

Her people.

How could she now think of beings who lived in the water as her people?

But she did. And since her arrival and the announcement of her betrothal to their king, all the werefins she had encountered had been friendly and had expressed pleasure at the joining.

Women's voices and laughter coming from the hallway outside the bedchamber had Kalina whirling around. To her delight, five women came rushing through the door. The Queens of Hearts, Spades, Diamonds and Clubs, along with Lady Abby of Oz.

Some disappointment settled in Kalina's belly that her friend Mikaela, the Queen of Malachad, would not be here. Kalina was certain Mikaela was not ready to face the queens she had almost killed when she was under Balin's mind-control.

She did not have time to dwell on it as the five women rushed to her and she hugged each one. Everyone was exclaiming and laughing so much that for a moment Kalina could not tell who was saying what. All five of the women were from a place called Earth, and their accents sometimes made it difficult for Kalina to understand them.

"Okay, give the woman room to breathe." The very pregnant Awai, the Queen of Clubs, held her hand to her large, round belly. "I could use some air, too," she added with a laugh.

Lady Abby of Oz tossed her red hair over her shoulder and grinned. "I know what Kalina must really enjoy about Eral. Talk about an orgasm of many colors." She turned to the queens. "I mean really. It's totally cool. When the woman fucks a werefin, her skin turns all the colors of the rainbow. It's supposed to be an amazing feeling." She gave a little pout. "Kir never would let me find out for myself."

Awai shook her head and Alexi laughed. Alice and Annie looked at each other, amusement on their features.

Kalina's cheeks heated for the first time in her life at the discussion of any kind of sex. She had probably experienced sexually everything a woman could until she met Eral. "Let us just say that you have not lived until you have experienced sex with a werefin."

Alexi, the redheaded Queen of Spades, cocked her head, her hands on her leather-clad hips. "This I've got to see. Can we watch, Kalina?"

Kalina's cheeks heated even more. "Ah..."

"Yeah, right." Pretty, blonde and full-figured Alice, the Queen of Hearts, gave a very unladylike snort to her twin sister Alexi. "As if Darronn would let you near any werefin much less Eral."

Alexi shrugged, but the light in her blue eyes was mischievous. "A girl can try."

The Queen of Diamonds, Annie, took Kalina's hands in hers and squeezed, her brown eyes meeting Kalina's. "Ignore them. You're about to be the Queen of Atlantis. This is a very special day."

"We've got something for you." Awai stepped forward and held out a swathe of cloth that shimmered like mother-of-pearl.

Annie released Kalina's hands. "We know you never wear clothes, but we thought maybe you'd like a little something for Eral to unwrap."

Alexi gave Kalina a once-over. "You're so beautiful that it's a shame to cover you up at all. But he's going to want you right away, so you might as well prolong his agony."

"Thank you." Kalina did not know what else to say except "It is breathtaking", as she took the silken cloth from Awai.

When she had it in her hands she saw that it was not only incredibly beautiful but that it was sheer and would accent her fair skin and dark hair. It would do nothing to hide her nipples or her quim.

"It's going to look perfect." Abby took the cloth from Kalina and started to help Kalina into it. "This is from Oz and you're going to love what this dress does to you. Eral gave me a similar one for our wedding."

Kalina raised a brow, but as soon as the ankle-length dress was on her she knew exactly what Abby was talking about. It adjusted to fit her as if she had been poured into it. But what was more was how it caressed her skin, as if hands were brushing her nipples and her quim, and she thought she was going to climax from the sensations. "Oh, my gods," she said, trying not to squirm in front of the women.

All five of them were now grinning at Kalina.

"Ohmigod is right." Alexi gave a small shiver and her breasts nearly spilled from the thin leather straps crisscrossing her chest and barely hiding her nipples. "We've had a chance to try on outfits made from that material and it's incredible."

"Magic." Alice smiled. "It's absolute magic."

The next moments were both excruciating and exciting to Kalina as she did her best not to climax from the sheer cloth that massaged her in such intimate ways.

The women sat her down on the bed and fussed with her hair. They finally decided to leave it down, but Awai braided tiny seed pearls into Kalina's hair on either side of her face. Annie, who was an artist, put what they called lipstick on Kalina's lips—the lipstick was a deep red color as was the blush Annie brushed on her cheeks. Next Annie rimmed Kalina's eyelids with kohl, then stepped back to look at her with an artist's critical eye.

"You didn't need a damn thing to make you any more gorgeous," Abby said with a shake of her head. "But that liner makes your eyes look even bigger and more beautiful."

"And with the blush and lipstick you're absolutely striking," Alice said in a breathless voice. "All the men are going to go even crazier than they normally do when you're around."

Kalina's cheeks were positively on fire. She was not used to such treatment or such profuse compliments.

When they finished, Alexi produced a small mirror from the pocket of her formfitting leather breeches. Kalina took a deep breath then held up the mirror to look at her reflection. Her lips parted in surprise at the change in her appearance. The makeup was subtle, yet accented her high cheekbones, her full lips and her amber eyes. The pearls woven into her hair shimmered in the chamber's soft lighting.

Before she could respond, the sound of a male clearing his throat came from the doorway. Kalina looked up to see Derel watching them and he seemed completely oblivious of his full erection. He was naked as all werefins chose to be when not in werefin form.

"Damnation, woman, Eral is the most fortunate of men. However you could always abandon him for me," he added with a teasing glint in his eyes and a wink.

Kalina smiled and the other women laughed.

"It is time." Derel held out his arm. Kalina went to him and slid her arm through his. He shook his head. "I am about to lose out on the most beautiful woman in Atlantis."

As they walked from the bedchamber toward the throne room, the other five women following, Kalina was surprised to find herself trembling. Derel gave her another teasing look, but then his smile was reassuring. "I feel blessed to have you as a sister, Kalina."

She returned his smile. "As I am to have you as a brother."

When they reached the throne room, little black spots danced before Kalina's eyes at the sight of so many people. Another first for her—she felt as though she might faint. But she smiled as she saw a tiny Lacos buzzing to land on Karney's shoulder.

Her gaze moved ahead and her heart gave a leap of joy when she saw the Kings of Tarok—Jarronn, the King of Hearts; Darronn, the King of Spades; Karn, the King of Diamonds; and Ty, the King of Clubs; along with Lord Kir of Oz. Each of these men she had loved in her own way, and she knew they loved her in return. She had shared her body with them, often at the same time, but she had never shared her heart and soul in the same way that she did with Eral. The fact that the kings, all weretigers, had braved the sea for her showed her even more how much they cared for her.

Derel escorted her past the males. Each king and lord gave her a smile and nod of pride and love as they were joined by their mates, the five women who had helped Kalina prepare for the joining. The women seemed just as proud as the men, no jealousy in their expressions whatsoever. They all knew Kalina's history of serving the kings in every way imaginable, yet they loved her, too.

When Kalina saw Eral standing at the foot of the two thrones, everyone and everything else ceased to exist.

She was barely aware of the sea of people, the cool polished floor beneath her feet, the caress of the dress against her skin from her shoulders to her ankles. What captured and held her attention was the man she was soon to be joined with, her mate for life. She had never believed she would be joined with one man. But she had discovered there was such a thing as love in her future.

Kalina no longer trembled when she reached Eral. Her eyes drank in his amazing blue eyes, his long silvery-blond hair that slid over his shoulders, and his more than perfect, naked physique. A crown of silver and pearls perched just above his brow and he looked so kingly he took her breath from her lungs. His cock jutted out proudly and her nipples tightened and quim grew wetter to know he wanted her. She almost wished he would take her in front of all of these people.

Derel slipped away, leaving her and Eral standing before what must have been most of the people in Atlantis.

"You are beyond beautiful, my love." Eral took her hands in his as his gaze traveled over her body from her toes to her eyes. "But what I love is your heart and soul."

"As I love you," she whispered.

Kalina suddenly became aware of Eral's mother, Navara. She was beside them, directly in front of the thrones, facing the people of Atlantis. She stood on one of the steps leading to the thrones and was just slightly higher than Kalina, but still Navara's head did not quite reach the height of Eral's.

In Navara's hands she held a crown that matched Eral's, only smaller. Eral's was perhaps a two-inch thick band around his head. The one that Navara held was about an inch wide, and as beautiful as Eral's.

Eral and Kalina turned to face Navara, their backs to the crowd.

"I am blessed to welcome into our family this child of the land," Navara said in a high, clear voice. "I am pleased to join my son, our king, Eral to Kalina of the weretigers." Navara's smile was soft, her eyes misty, as she raised her hands and held the crown over Kalina's head. "I am proud to call Kalina my daughter, and our queen."

Kalina shivered, her skin pricking with goose bumps as Navara set the crown upon Kalina's head. It fit perfectly, sitting just above her brow. She gave a bow from her shoulders to Eral's mother and as she raised her head, her eyes met Navara's. The woman smiled and Kalina could see that the pride in her eyes was genuine.

Navara's voice again rang loud and clear as she addressed the crowd. "I present to you the King and Queen of Atlantis."

As one Eral and Kalina turned to the crowd. He gripped her hand tight as cheers and clapping broke out, so loud that the room reverberated with it.

Eral caught Kalina's face in his hands and brought her around to face him again. "My Queen," he said in his deep voice.

Kalina trembled within his grip. "My King."

Eral captured her mouth in a dominant, possessive kiss. "Mine," he said urgently against her lips. "Forever mine."

It seemed as though the celebration lasted for ages before Eral took Kalina by the hand and they slipped away to their bedchamber.

"How could you tease me so?" Eral pinched her nipples through the fabric that had never ceased torturing her. "To hide your body from me in any way."

Kalina could only say, "I want you, Eral. I need you."

He dipped his head to suckle one of her nipples through the thin fabric at the same time he cupped her cloth-covered mound. Kalina grasped him by his shoulders and cried out. "Oh, gods." The torture increased tenfold. Yet somehow she knew the fabric would not let her climax no matter how close her body came to the peak. It had been so the entire night.

Eral bit her nipple, causing her to cry out at the pleasure of it. He laved the taut bud before turning his attention to her other breast, giving it the same attention.

"We must get this off you," he said in what could only be called a demand. He tried sliding it down her shoulders, tried pulling at the fabric. "How do you remove this godsdamn thing?"

"I do not know," Kalina said as she looked up at him. "Just get it off, I do not care how."

Eral grasped the front of the material in his fists. His jaw was tense, his eyes blue fire as his biceps bulged. In one quick movement he shredded the material and flung it away from her so that it landed in a shimmering heap on the polished floor.

He scooped her up within his powerful arms, causing her to cry out and wrap her arms around his neck. "Do not ever cover your body from me again," he commanded.

She could not take her eyes from his. "Yes, my King."

They fell onto the bed together, their bodies sliding on the satiny sheets. Eral quickly drew her beneath him, his hips hard between her spread thighs, his cock pressed to her wet folds.

For a long time he looked down at her. "From the moment I saw you, I knew you were mine."

Kalina could not find her voice at first. She swallowed as her thoughts reeled back to when they first met and how she had avoided him. "I think my heart knew it, too," she said slowly. "I just did not believe it. Did not believe that I could ever find love."

His face was serious as his long hair brushed her nipples. "You were meant for me, Kalina. Only for me."

She nodded, her hair sliding against the satin of the bed coverings. "As you were meant for me."

Eral's expression remained serious as he lowered his face to hers until their noses were touching and their eyes were locked. "I love you, Kalina. I always will."

At the same time he brought his mouth to hers, he slid his cock into her wet quim. Kalina moaned at the sensation of him easing in and out as he made love to her. His tongue gently met hers as he filled her...body, mind, heart and soul. The moment was so beautiful that a tear trickled from the corners of her eyes.

When he drew back to look at her, he never stopped the slow, rocking motion of his hips. Without a word he dipped his head down to trace the path of one of her tears with his tongue, then did the same with her other eye.

He kept up the pace that was bringing her closer to climax. Everything was so precious that her body filled with so much emotion that she could no longer contain it. "Eral, please come with me. I will not go without you."

His thrusts became harder, more powerful. Their eyes remained locked as Kalina got lost in the depths of his blue eyes.

"Now," he said as he buried himself deep, deep within her.

All the emotion and love she had kept stored within her burst from her, and her cry rang through the room, joined by his. The colors of her orgasm slid beneath her skin, but she saw them in her mind, too. Rippling like a rainbow followed by brilliant white stars.

She felt the pulse of his cock within her, the contractions of her core around him as his seed filled her.

Eral withdrew his cock from Kalina and cradled her in his arms. He moved them both so that he was on his back and she was snuggled in the crook of his arm, her head lying on his chest so that she heard the steady pounding of his heart.

"That is for you," he murmured and she heard the power in his voice rumble in his chest. "My heart beats for you."

Kalina sighed as she relaxed in Eral's arms. "I am home now," she said. "I have finally found my home with you."

Also by Cheyenne McCray

❦

Blackstar: Future Knight

Castaways

Ellora's Cavemen: Season's of Seduction II (*anthology*)

Ellora's Cavemen: Tales from the Temple III (*anthology*)

Erotic Invitation

Erotic Stranger

Erotic Weekend

Hearts Are Wild (*anthology*)

Return to Wonderland: Lord Kir of Oz *with Mackenzie McKade*

Seraphine Chronicles 1: Bewitched

Seraphine Chronicles 2: Forbidden

Seraphine Chronicles 3: Spellbound

Seraphine Chronicles 4: Untamed

Stranger in My Stocking

Taboo: Taking Instruction

Taboo: Taking It Personal

Taboo: Taking On the Law

Taboo: Taking the Job

Things That Go Bump in the Night 3 (*anthology*)

Vampire Dreams *with Annie Windsor*

Wild 1: Wild Borders

Wild 2: Wildcard

Wild 3: Wildcat

Wild 4: Wildfire

Wonderland 1: King of Clubs

Wonderland 2: King of Diamonds

Wonderland 3: King of Hearts

Wonderland 4: King of Spades

Also by Mackenzie McKade

෨

A Tall, Dark Cowboy
Echoes from Heaven
Ecstacy: Forbidden Fruit
Ecstacy: The Charade
Ecstacy: The Game
Return to Wonderland: Lord Kir of Oz *with Cheyenne McCray*
White Hot Holidays: A Very Faery Christmas

About the Authors

ຂວ

USA Today Bestselling Author Cheyenne McCray has a passion for sensual romance and a happily-ever-after, but always with a twist. Among other accolades, Chey has been presented with the prestigious Romantic Times BOOK reviews Reviewers' Choice Award for "Best Erotic Romance of the Year". Chey is the award-winning novelist of eighteen books and nine novellas.

Chey has been writing ever since she can remember, back to her kindergarten days when she penned her first poem. She always knew one day she would write novels, hoping her readers would get lost in the worlds she created, as she did when she was lost in a good book. Cheyenne enjoys spending time with her husband and three sons, traveling, and of course writing, writing, writing.

A taste of the erotic, a measure of daring and a hint of laughter describes Mackenzie McKade's novels. She sizzles the pages with scorching sex, fantasy and deep emotion that will touch you and keep you immersed until the end. Whether her stories are contemporaries, futuristics or fantasies, this Arizona native thrives on giving you the ultimate erotic adventure.

When not traveling through her vivid imagination, she's spending time with three beautiful daughters, a devilishly handsome grandson, and the man of her dreams. She loves to write, enjoys reading, and can't wait 'til summer. Boating and jet skiing are top on her list of activities. Add to that laughter and if mischief is in order—Mackenzie's your gal!

Cheyenne and Mackenzie welcomes comments from readers. You can find their website and email address on their author bio page at www.ellorascave.com.

Tell Us What You Think

We appreciate hearing reader opinions about our books. You can email us at Comments@EllorasCave.com.

Why an electronic book?

We live in the Information Age — an exciting time in the history of human civilization, in which technology rules supreme and continues to progress in leaps and bounds every minute of every day. For a multitude of reasons, more and more avid literary fans are opting to purchase e-books instead of paper books. The question from those not yet initiated into the world of electronic reading is simply: *Why?*

1. *Price.* An electronic title at Ellora's Cave Publishing and Cerridwen Press runs anywhere from 40% to 75% less than the cover price of the exact same title in paperback format. Why? Basic mathematics and cost. It is less expensive to publish an e-book (no paper and printing, no warehousing and shipping) than it is to publish a paperback, so the savings are passed along to the consumer.

2. *Space.* Running out of room in your house for your books? That is one worry you will never have with electronic books. For a low one-time cost, you can purchase a handheld device specifically designed for e-reading. Many e-readers have large, convenient screens for viewing. Better yet, hundreds of titles can be stored within your new library — on a single microchip. There are a variety of e-readers from different manufacturers. You can also read e-books on your PC or laptop computer. (Please note that Ellora's Cave does not endorse any specific brands.

You can check our websites at www.elloracave.com or www.cerridwenpress.com for information we make available to new consumers.)

3. *Mobility.* Because your new e-library consists of only a microchip within a small, easily transportable e-reader, your entire cache of books can be taken with you wherever you go.

4. *Personal Viewing Preferences.* Are the words you are currently reading too small? Too large? Too… ANNOYING? Paperback books cannot be modified according to personal preferences, but e-books can.

5. *Instant Gratification.* Is it the middle of the night and all the bookstores near you are closed? Are you tired of waiting days, sometimes weeks, for bookstores to ship the novels you bought? Ellora's Cave Publishing sells instantaneous downloads twenty-four hours a day, seven days a week, every day of the year. Our webstore is never closed. Our e-book delivery system is 100% automated, meaning your order is filled as soon as you pay for it.

Those are a few of the top reasons why electronic books are replacing paperbacks for many avid readers.

As always, Ellora's Cave and Cerridwen Press welcome your questions and comments. We invite you to email us at Comments@ellorascave.com or write to us directly at Ellora's Cave Publishing Inc., 1056 Home Avenue, Akron, OH 44310-3502.

COMING TO A BOOKSTORE NEAR YOU!

ELLORA'S CAVE

Bestselling Authors Tour

Cerridwen, the Celtic Goddess of wisdom, was the muse who brought inspiration to storytellers and those in the creative arts. Cerridwen Press encompasses the best and most innovative stories in all genres of today's fiction. Visit our site and discover the newest titles by talented authors who still get inspired - much like the ancient storytellers did, once upon a time.

Cerridwen Press

www.cerridwenpress.com